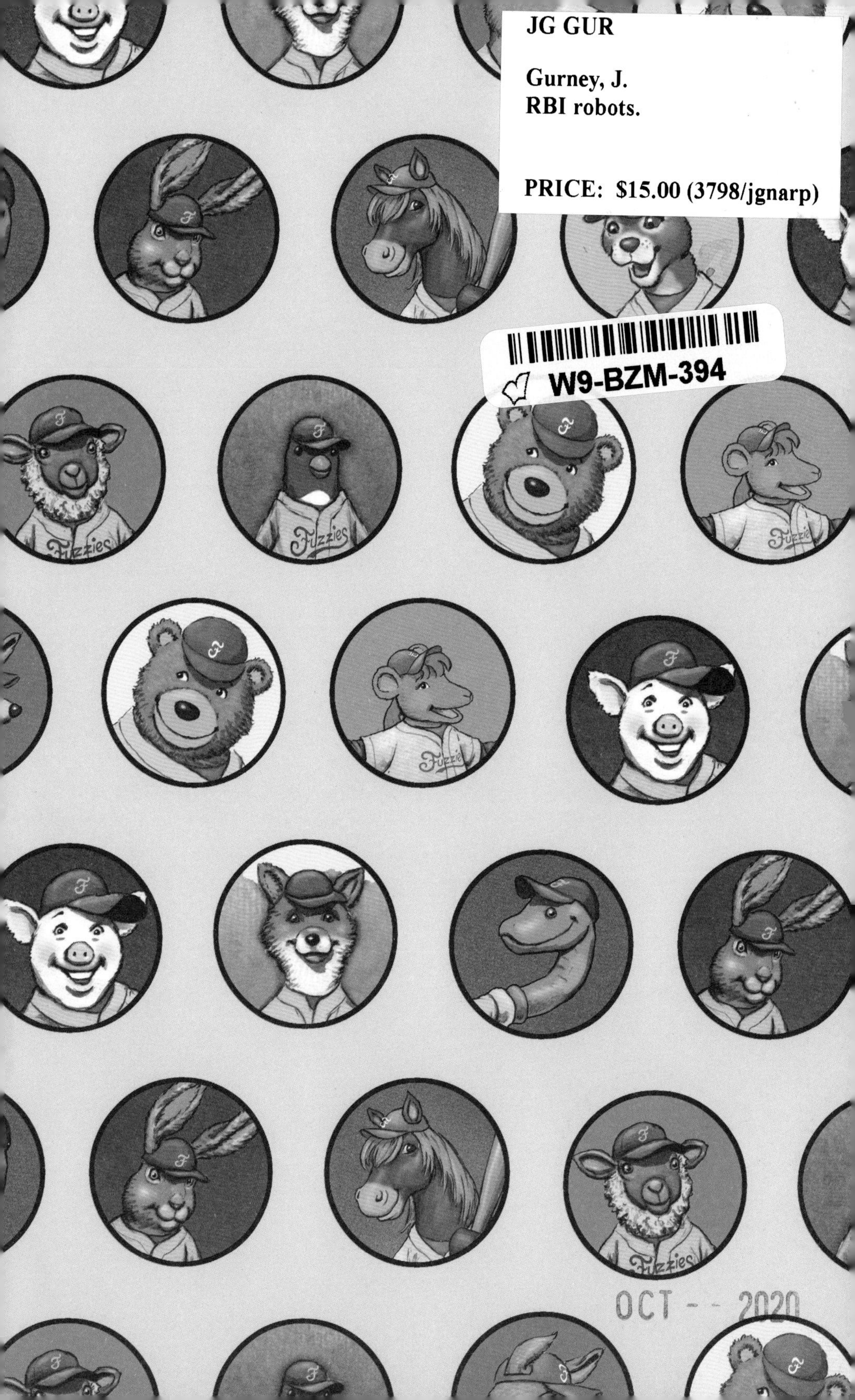
Fuzzies

Fuzzy Baseball

3

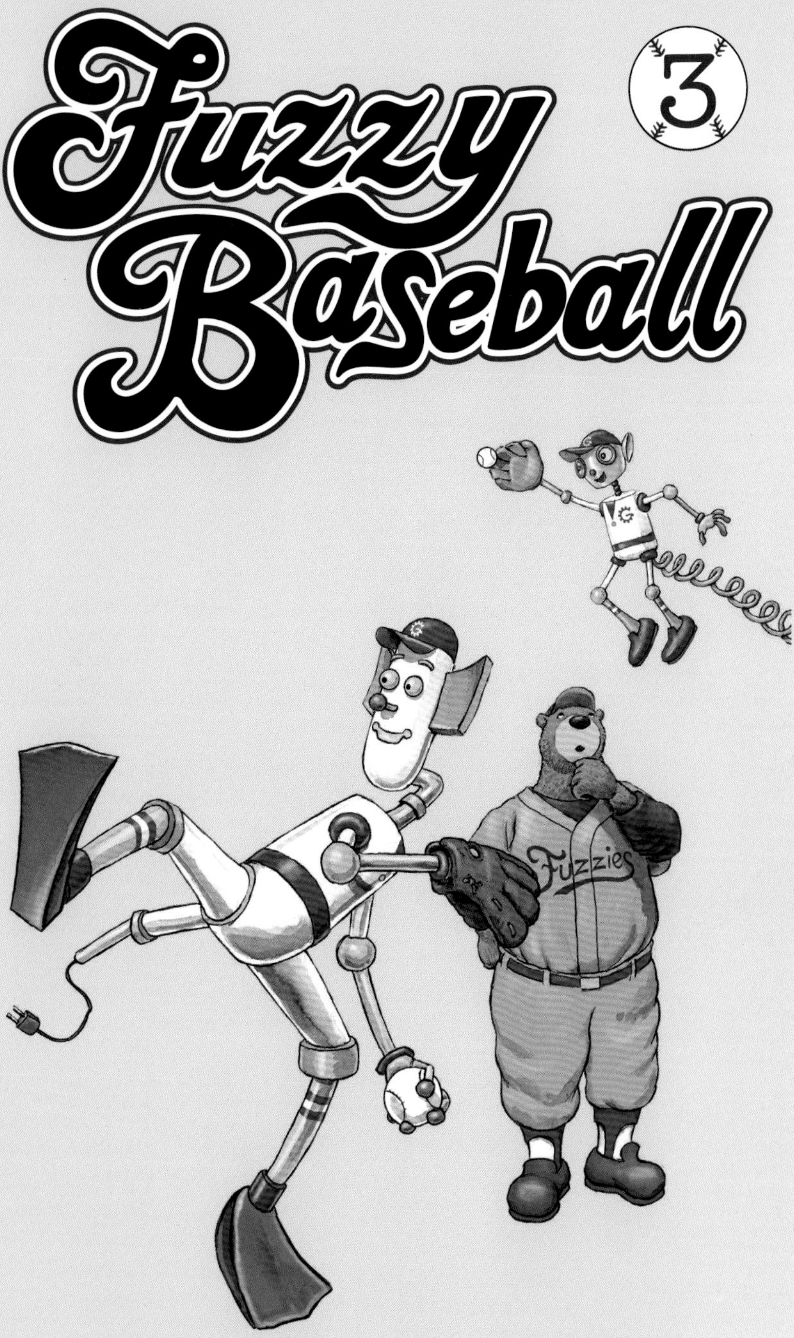
Fuzzies

John Steven Gurney

PAPERCUTZ

To my buddy Leo, the Official Baseball Consultant for the
FUZZY BASEBALL Series. And to Kathie.

Fuzzy Baseball #3
"RBI Robots"
Created by JOHN STEVEN GURNEY
JAYJAY JACKSON—Production
JEFF WHITMAN—Managing Editor
JIM SALICRUP
Editor-in-Chief

Hardcover ISBN: 978-1-5458-0476-6
Paperback ISBN: 978-1-5458-0475-9

Printed in China
May 2019

Papercutz books may be purchased for
business or promotional use.
For information on bulk purchases please contact
Macmillan Corporate and Premium Sales Department at
(800) 221-795 x5442.

Distributed by Macmillan
First printing

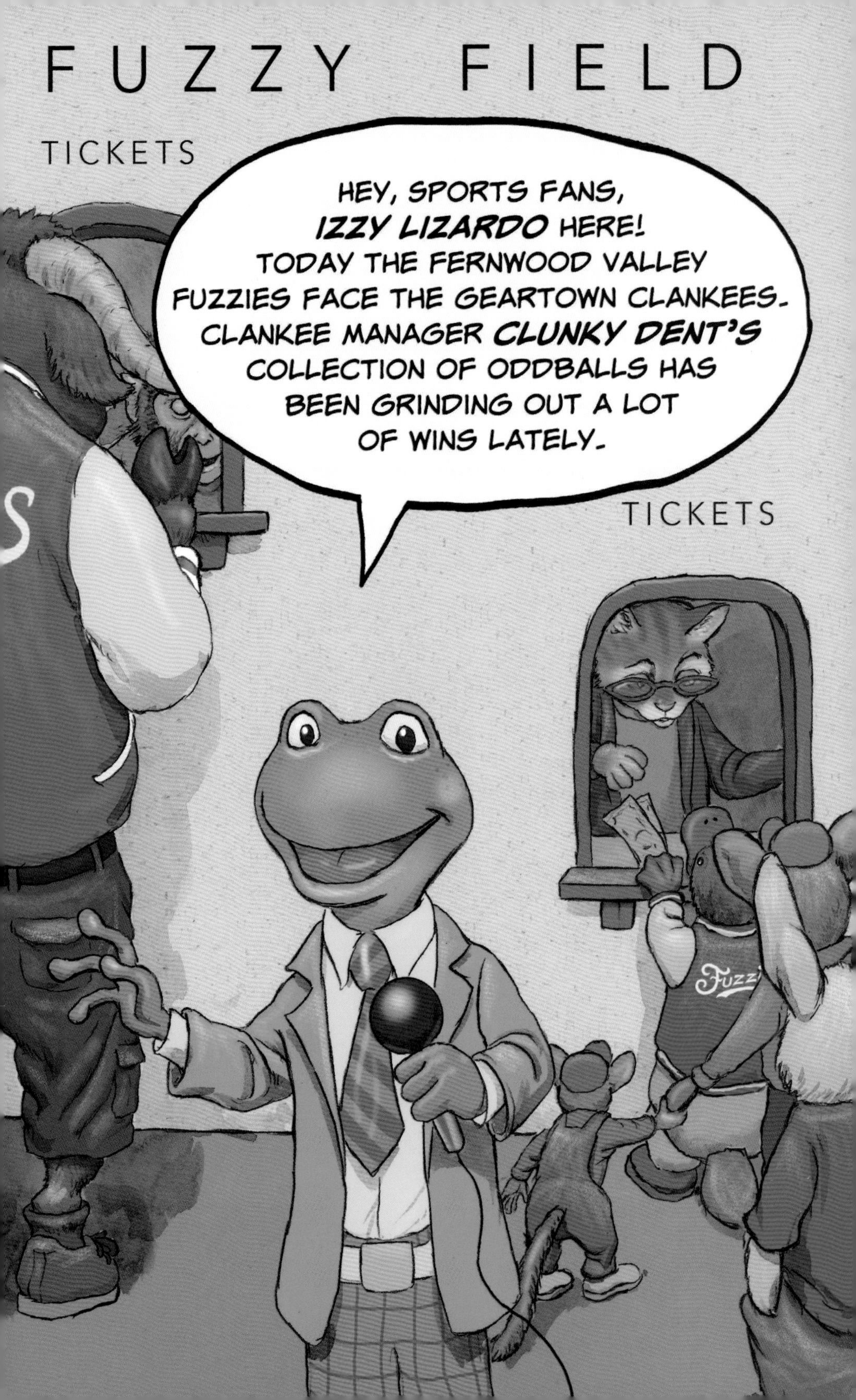
FUZZY FIELD
TICKETS
HEY, SPORTS FANS, IZZY LIZARDO HERE! TODAY THE FERNWOOD VALLEY FUZZIES FACE THE GEARTOWN CLANKEES. CLANKEE MANAGER CLUNKY DENT'S COLLECTION OF ODDBALLS HAS BEEN GRINDING OUT A LOT OF WINS LATELY.
TICKETS

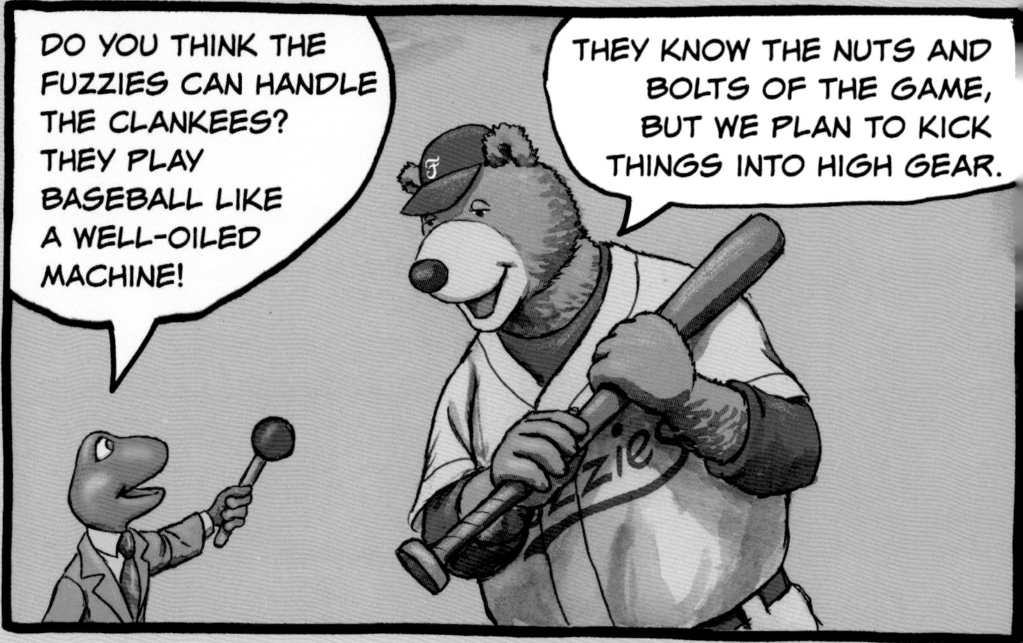
DO YOU THINK THE FUZZIES CAN HANDLE THE CLANKEES? THEY PLAY BASEBALL LIKE A WELL-OILED MACHINE!
THEY KNOW THE NUTS AND BOLTS OF THE GAME, BUT WE PLAN TO KICK THINGS INTO HIGH GEAR.

INTRODUCING THE GEARTOWN CLANKEES...

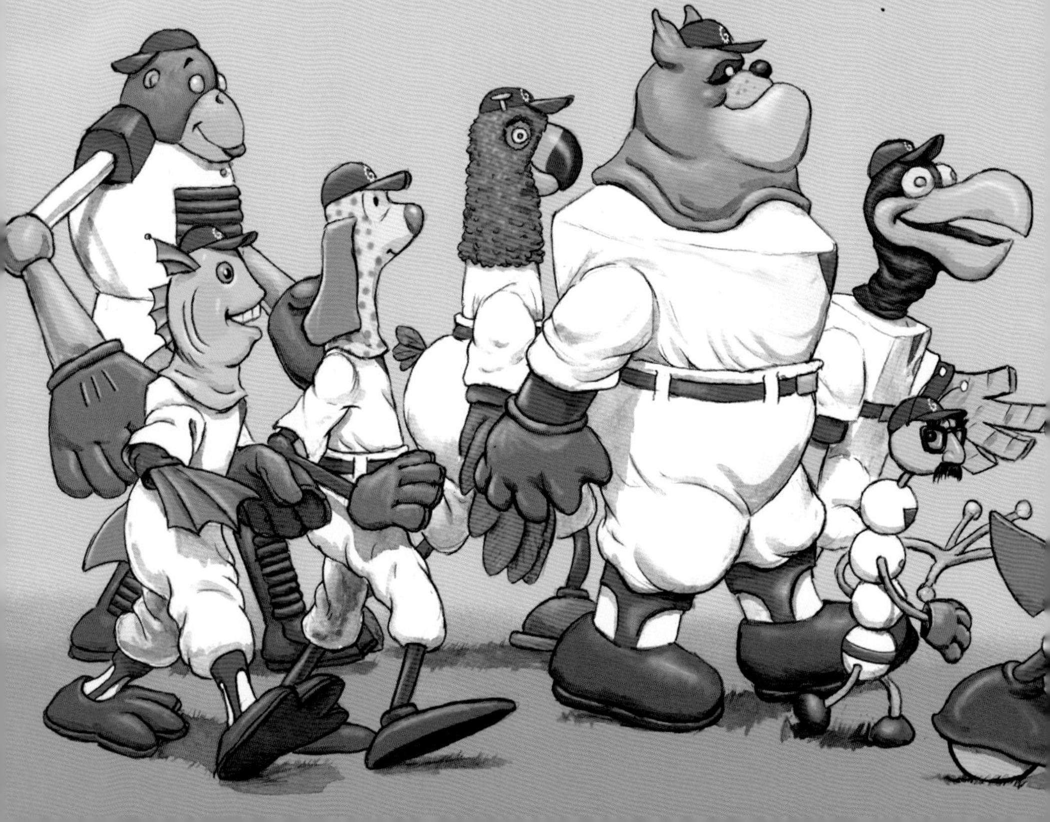

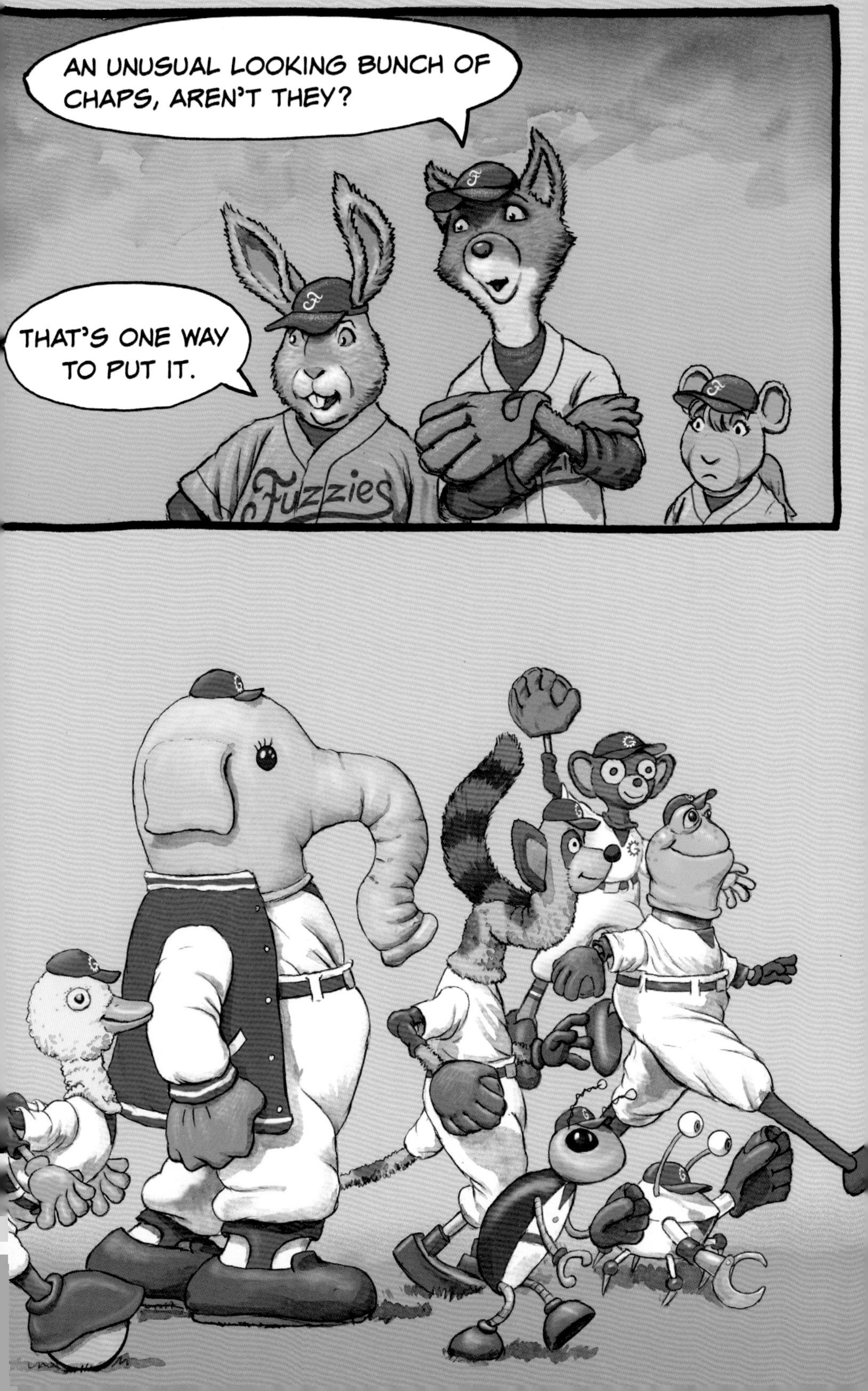
AN UNUSUAL LOOKING BUNCH OF CHAPS, AREN'T THEY?
THAT'S ONE WAY TO PUT IT.
Fuzzies

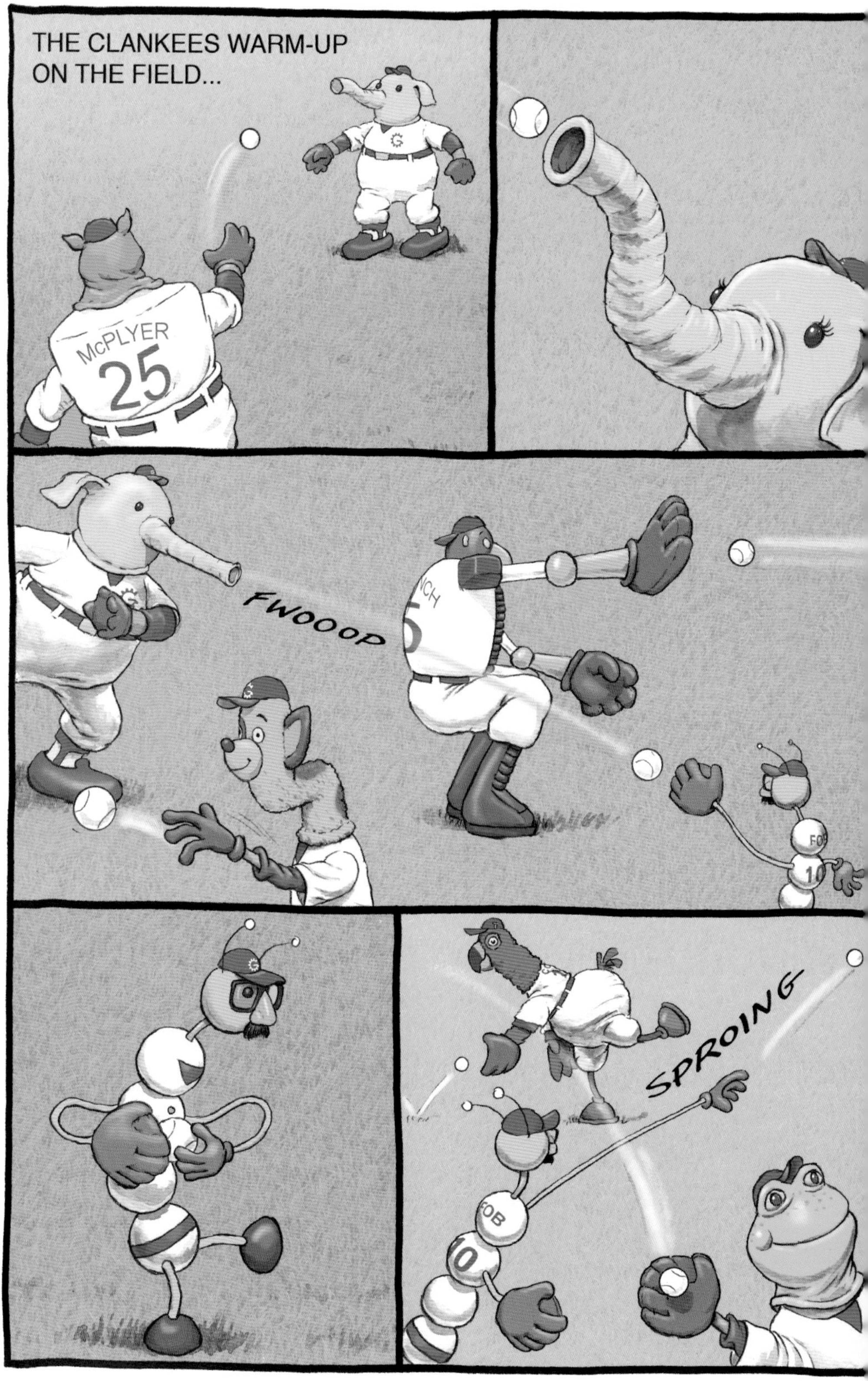
THE CLANKEES WARM-UP ON THE FIELD...
McPLYER
25
FWOOOP
SPROING
FOB
10

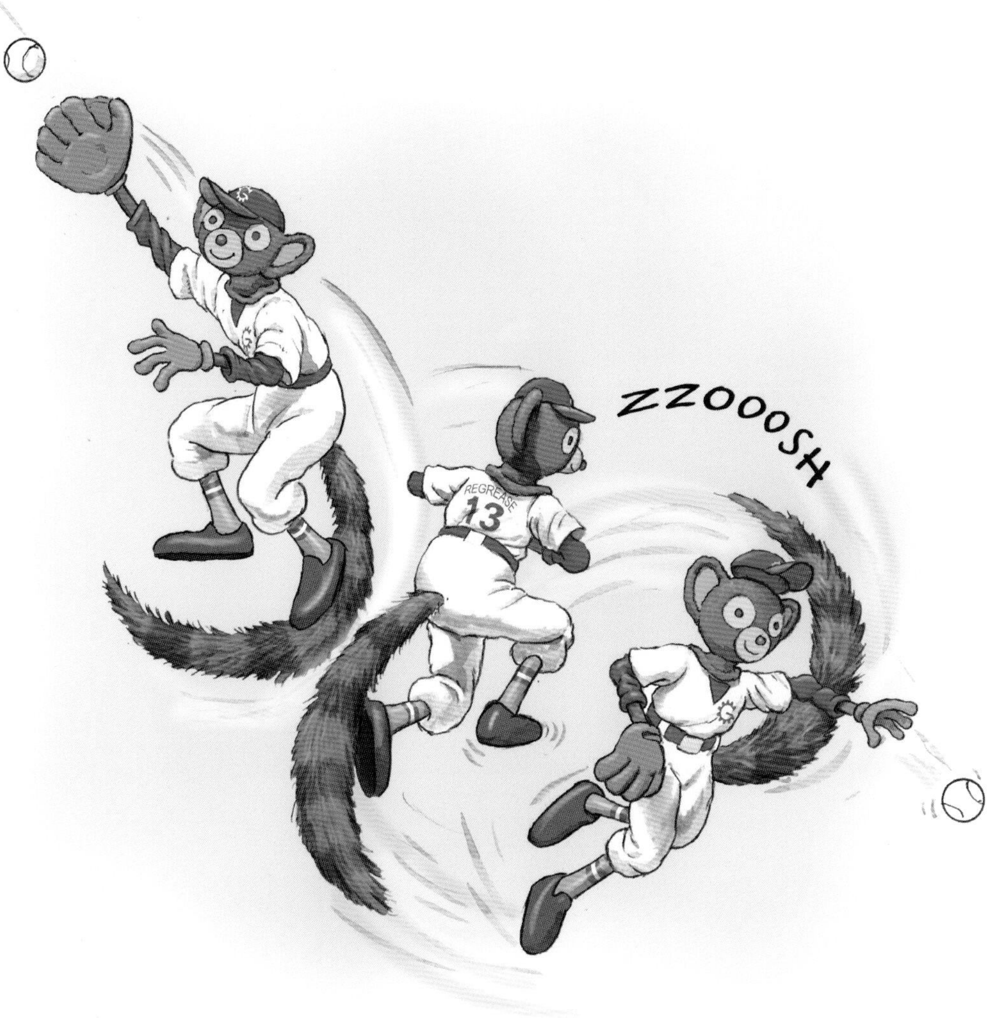
REGREASE
13
ZZOOOOSH

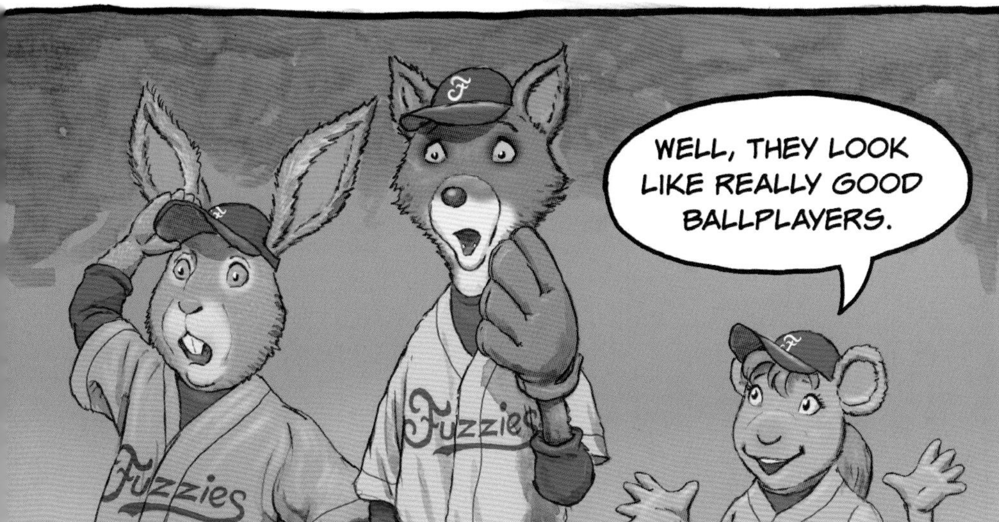
WELL, THEY LOOK LIKE REALLY GOOD BALLPLAYERS.
Fuzzies
Fuzzies

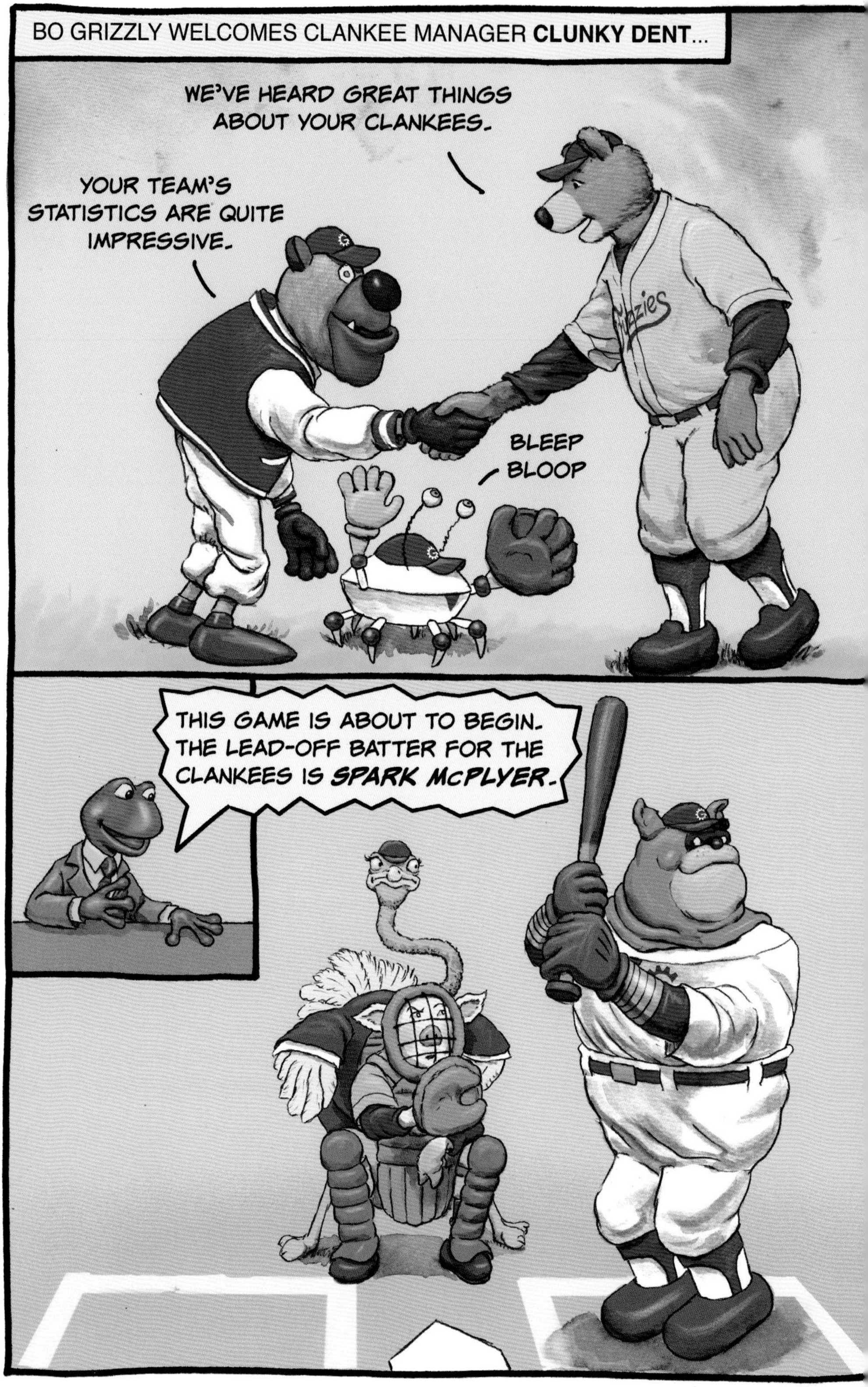
BO GRIZZLY WELCOMES CLANKEE MANAGER **CLUNKY DENT**...
WE'VE HEARD GREAT THINGS ABOUT YOUR CLANKEES.
YOUR TEAM'S STATISTICS ARE QUITE IMPRESSIVE.
BLEEP BLOOP
THIS GAME IS ABOUT TO BEGIN. THE LEAD-OFF BATTER FOR THE CLANKEES IS *SPARK McPLYER*.

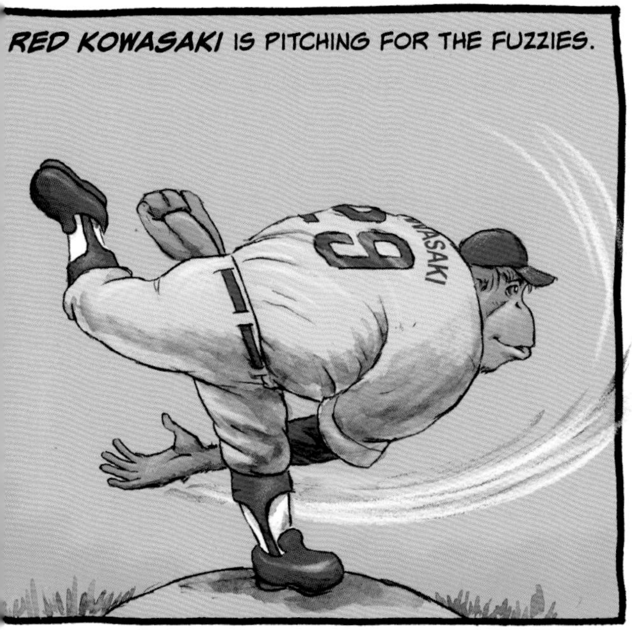
RED KOWASAKI IS PITCHING FOR THE FUZZIES.
69
KOWASAKI

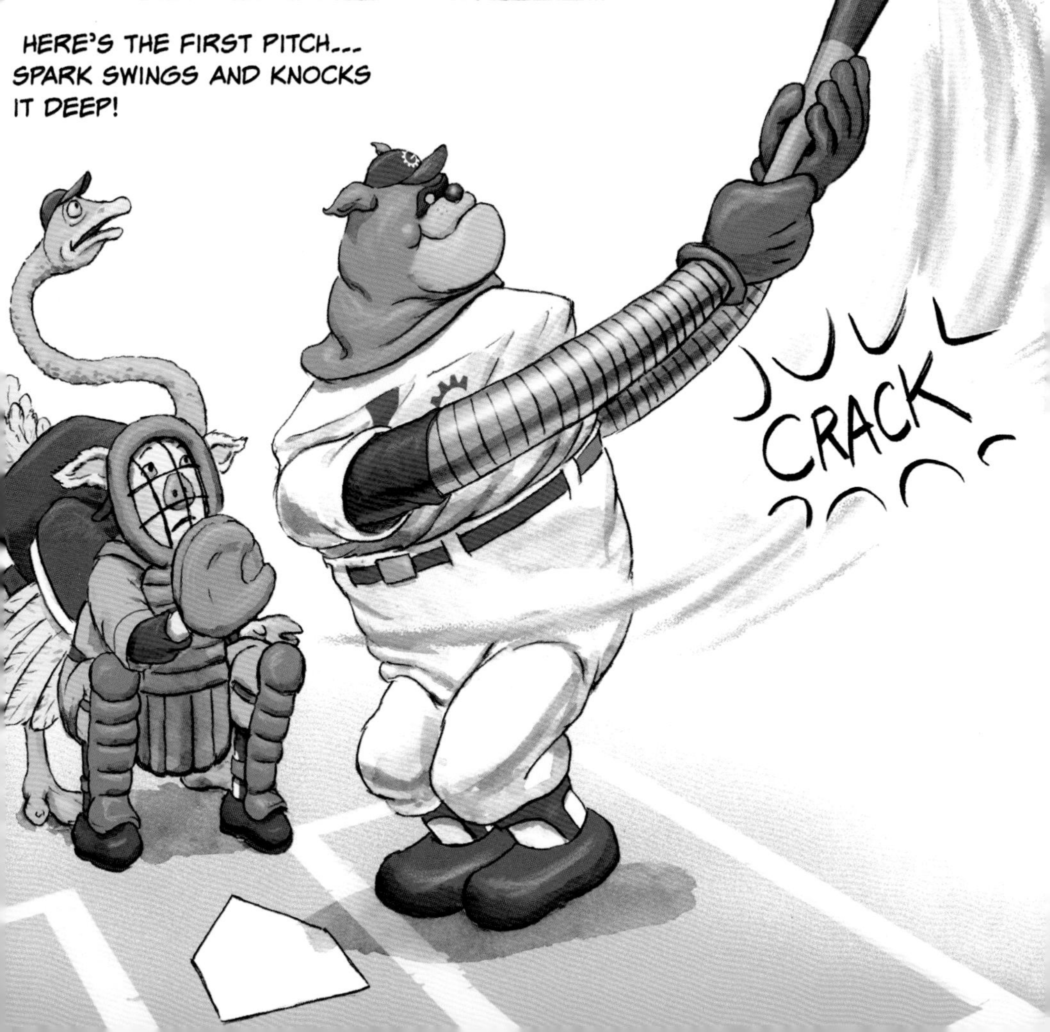
HERE'S THE FIRST PITCH...
SPARK SWINGS AND KNOCKS
IT DEEP!
CRACK

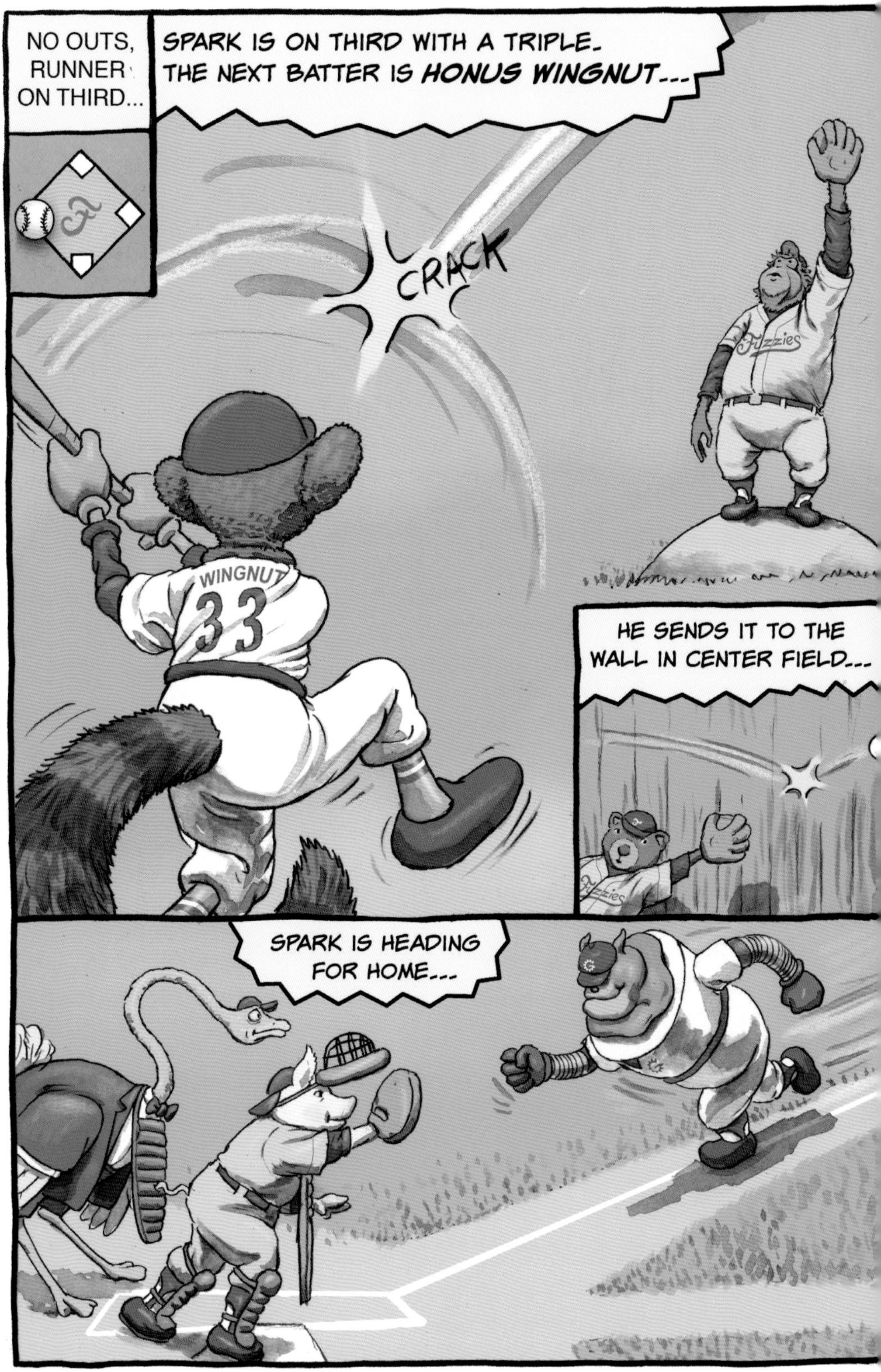
NO OUTS, RUNNERS ON THIRD...
SPARK IS ON THIRD WITH A TRIPLE. THE NEXT BATTER IS *HONUS WINGNUT*...
CRACK
WINGNUT 33
Fuzzies
HE SENDS IT TO THE WALL IN CENTER FIELD...
SPARK IS HEADING FOR HOME...

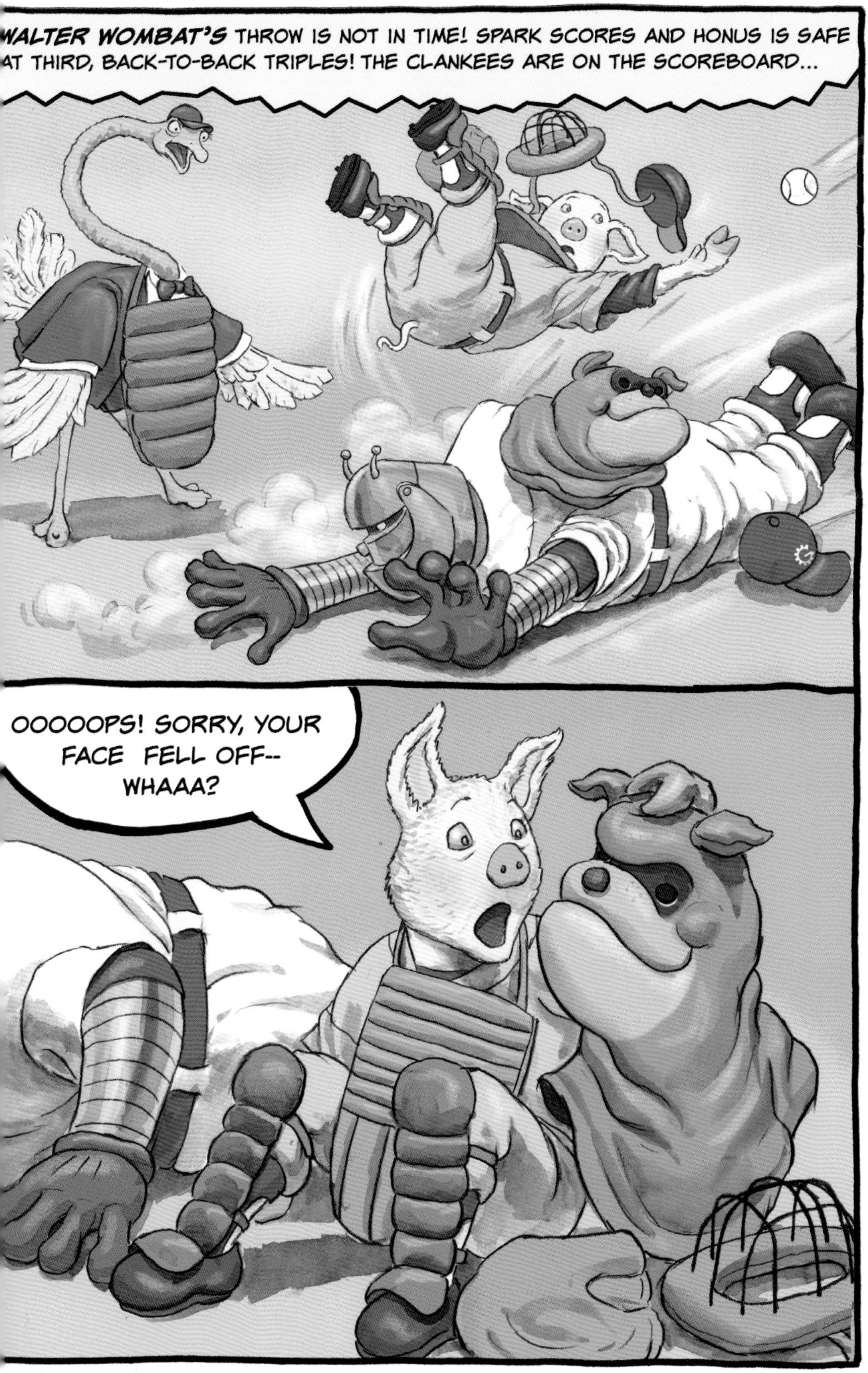
WALTER WOMBAT'S THROW IS NOT IN TIME! SPARK SCORES AND HONUS IS SAFE AT THIRD, BACK-TO-BACK TRIPLES! THE CLANKEES ARE ON THE SCOREBOARD...
OOOOOPS! SORRY, YOUR FACE FELL OFF-- WHAAA?

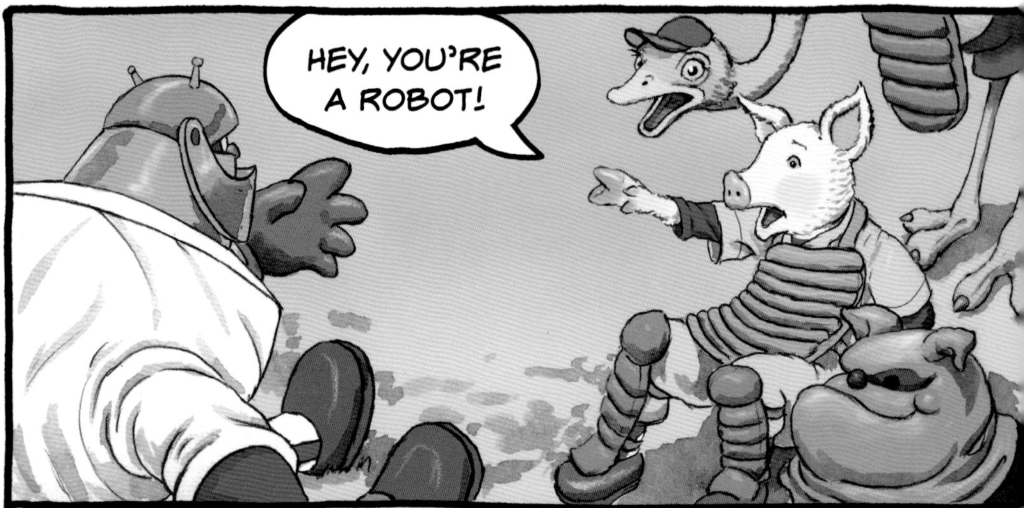
HEY, YOU'RE A ROBOT!

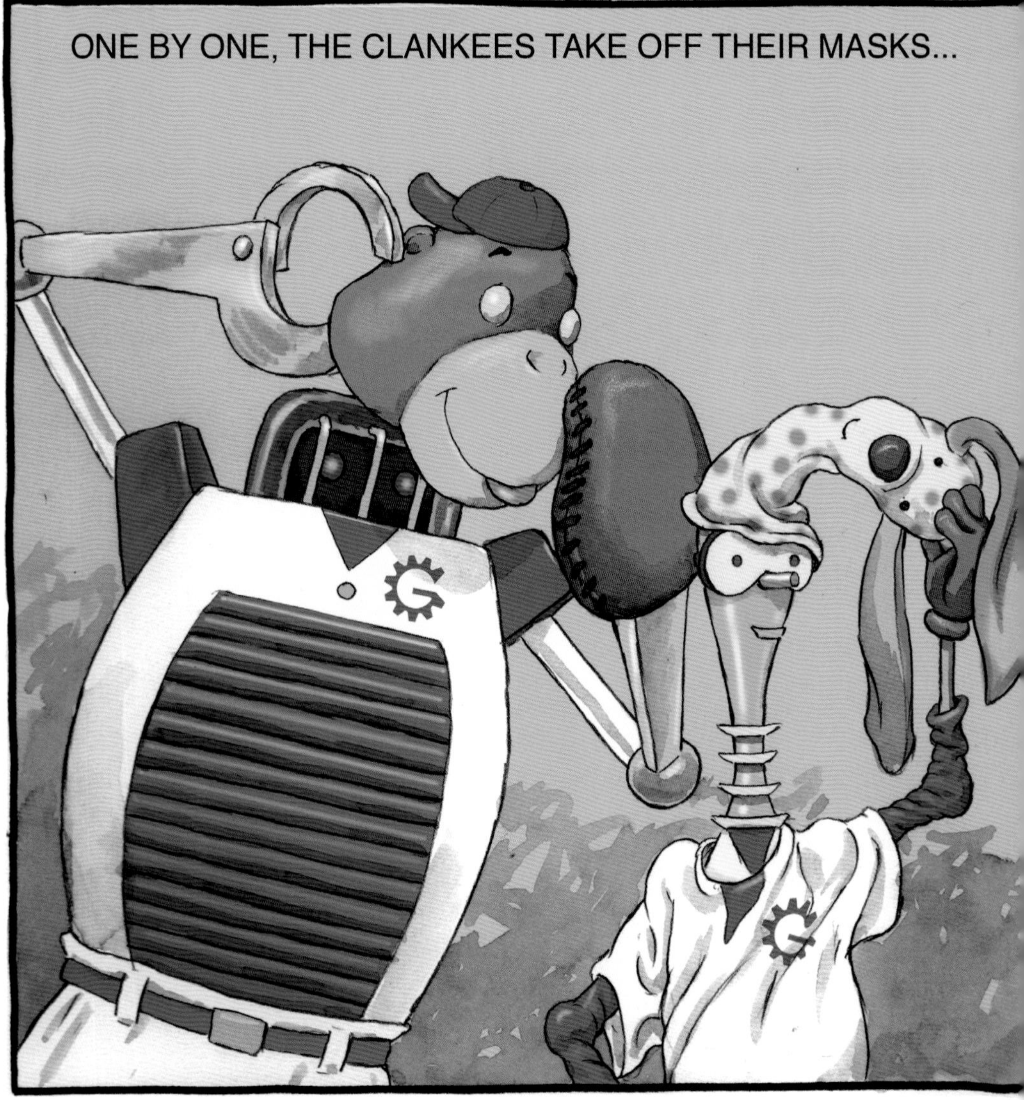
ONE BY ONE, THE CLANKEES TAKE OFF THEIR MASKS...

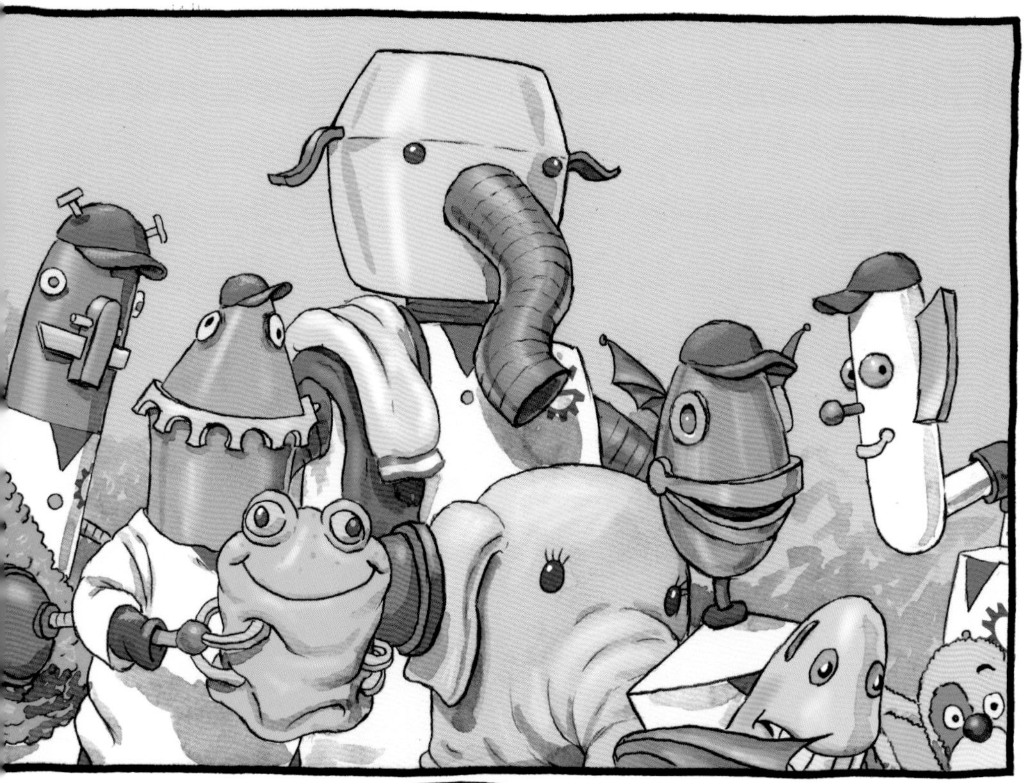

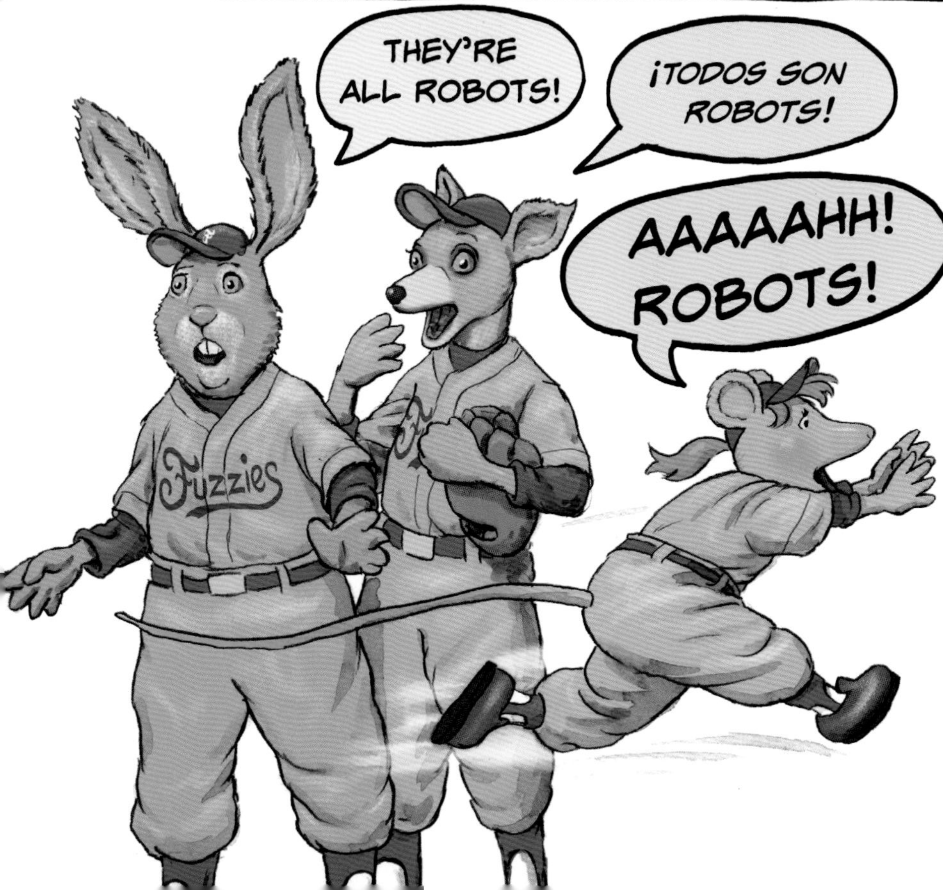
THEY'RE ALL ROBOTS!
¡TODOS SON ROBOTS!
AAAAAHH! ROBOTS!
Fuzzies

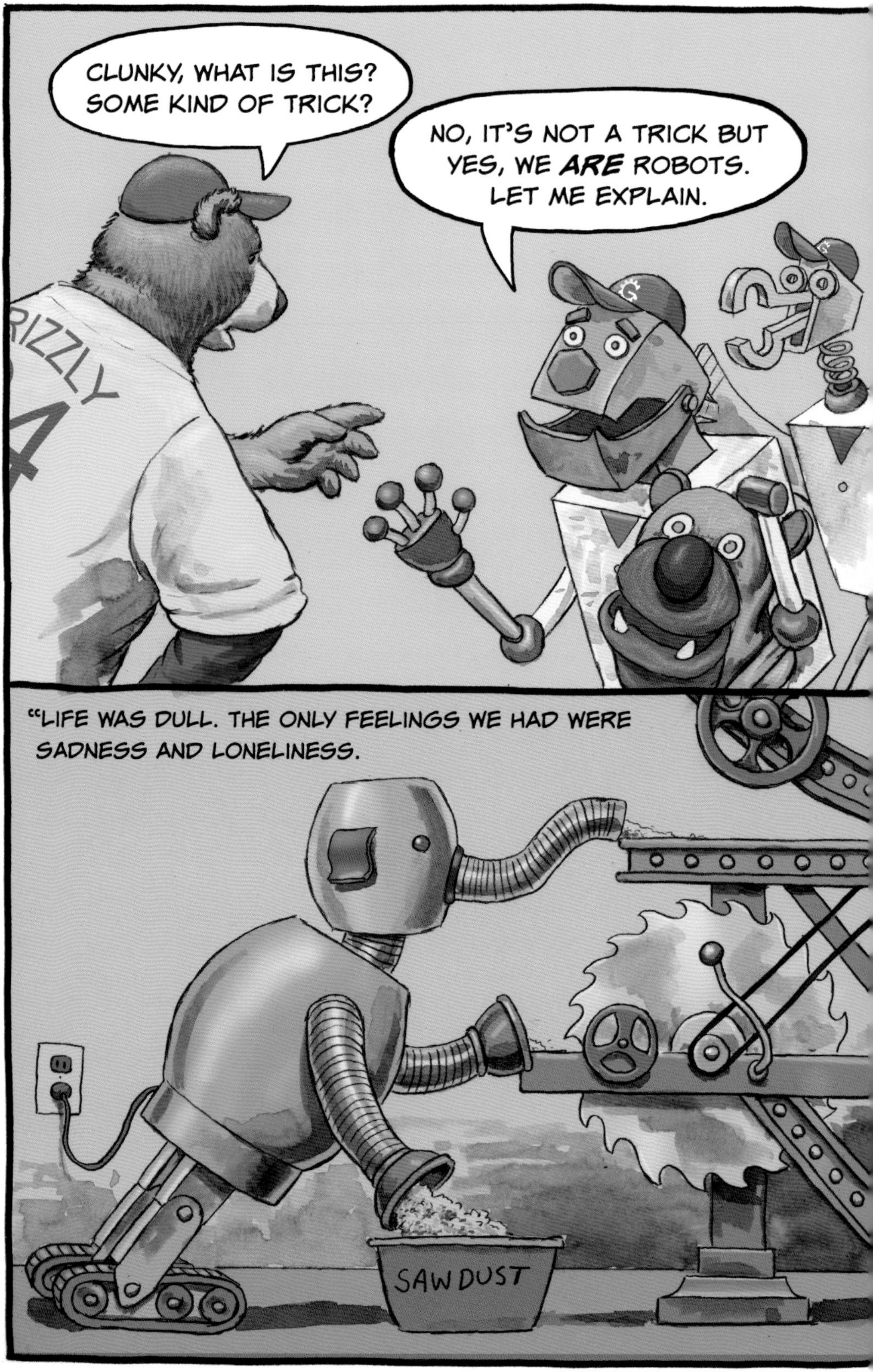
CLUNKY, WHAT IS THIS? SOME KIND OF TRICK?
NO, IT'S NOT A TRICK BUT YES, WE ARE ROBOTS. LET ME EXPLAIN.
"LIFE WAS DULL. THE ONLY FEELINGS WE HAD WERE SADNESS AND LONELINESS.
SAWDUST

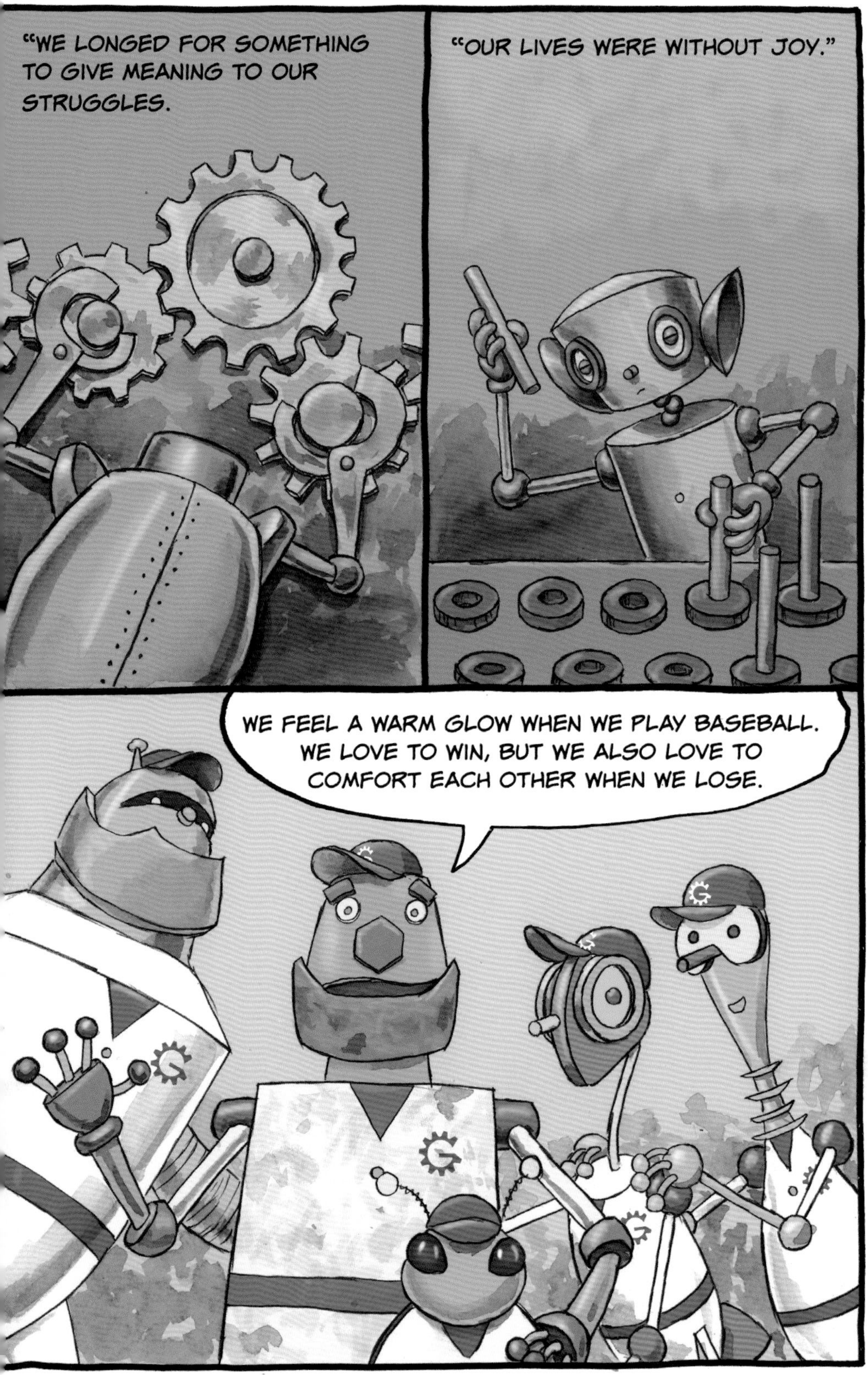
"WE LONGED FOR SOMETHING TO GIVE MEANING TO OUR STRUGGLES.
"OUR LIVES WERE WITHOUT JOY."
WE FEEL A WARM GLOW WHEN WE PLAY BASEBALL. WE LOVE TO WIN, BUT WE ALSO LOVE TO COMFORT EACH OTHER WHEN WE LOSE.

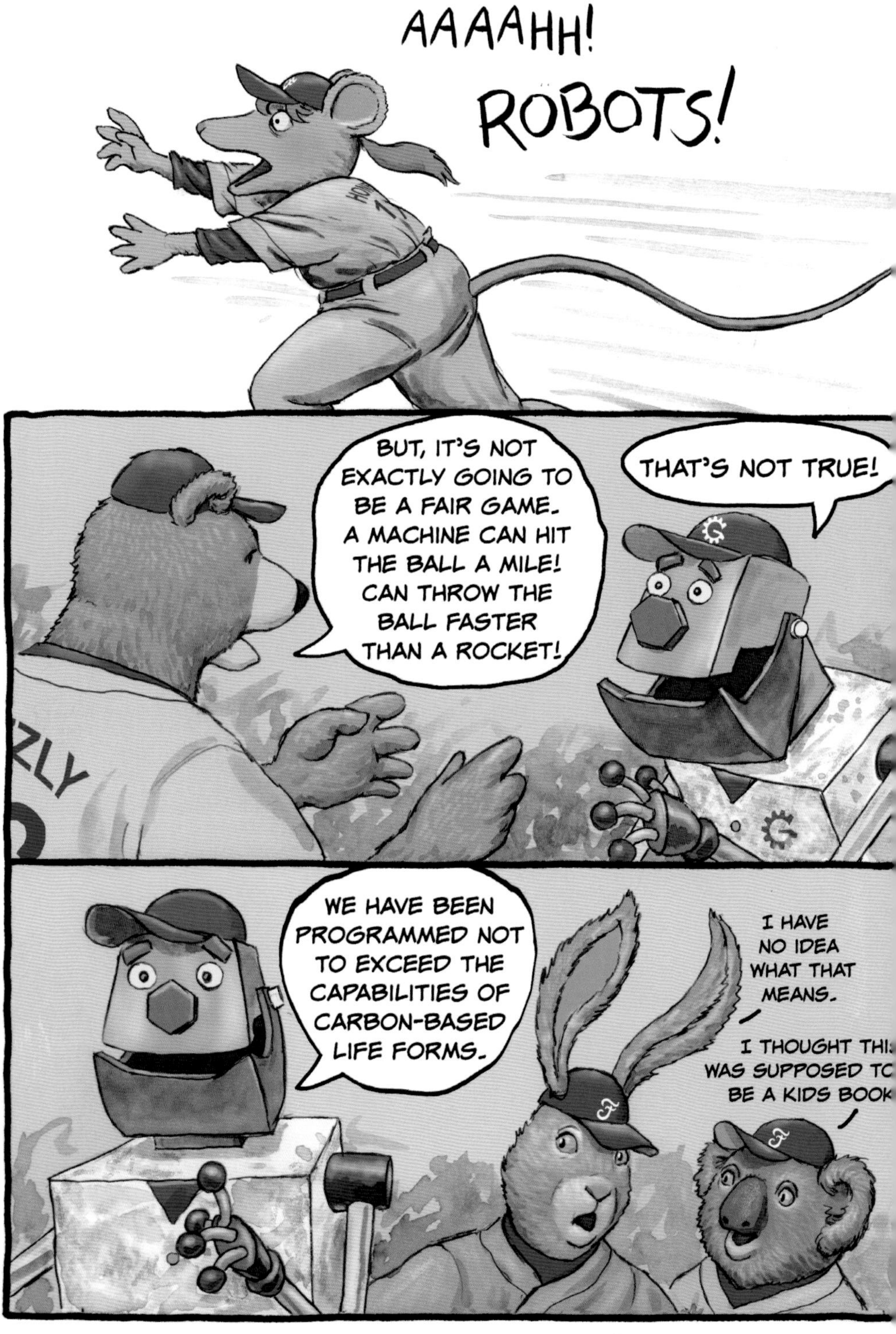
AAAAHH!
ROBOTS!
BUT, IT'S NOT EXACTLY GOING TO BE A FAIR GAME. A MACHINE CAN HIT THE BALL A MILE! CAN THROW THE BALL FASTER THAN A ROCKET!
THAT'S NOT TRUE!
WE HAVE BEEN PROGRAMMED NOT TO EXCEED THE CAPABILITIES OF CARBON-BASED LIFE FORMS.
I HAVE NO IDEA WHAT THAT MEANS.
I THOUGHT THI
WAS SUPPOSED T
BE A KIDS BOOK

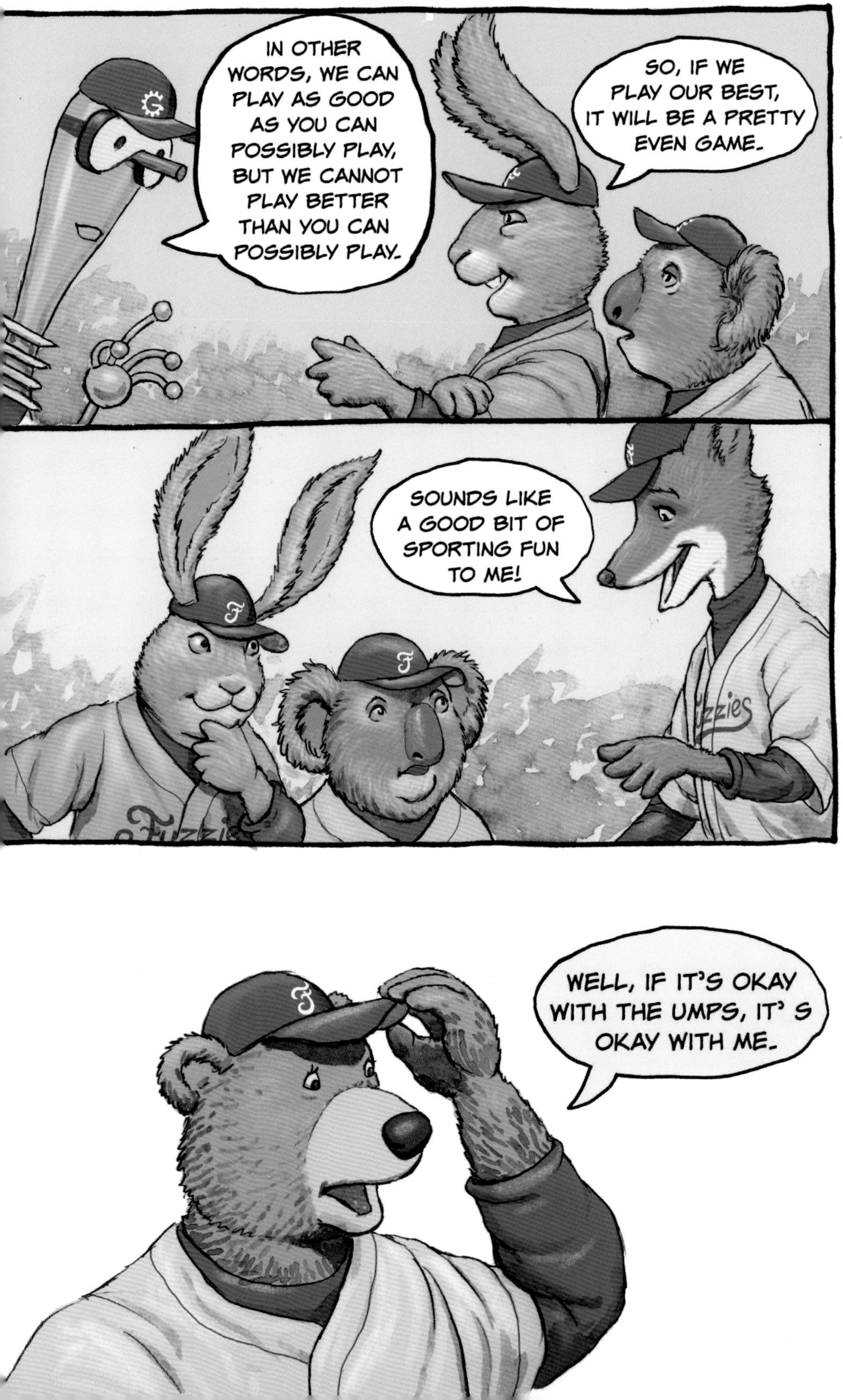
IN OTHER WORDS, WE CAN PLAY AS GOOD AS YOU CAN POSSIBLY PLAY, BUT WE CANNOT PLAY BETTER THAN YOU CAN POSSIBLY PLAY.
SO, IF WE PLAY OUR BEST, IT WILL BE A PRETTY EVEN GAME.
SOUNDS LIKE A GOOD BIT OF SPORTING FUN TO ME!
WELL, IF IT'S OKAY WITH THE UMPS, IT' S OKAY WITH ME.

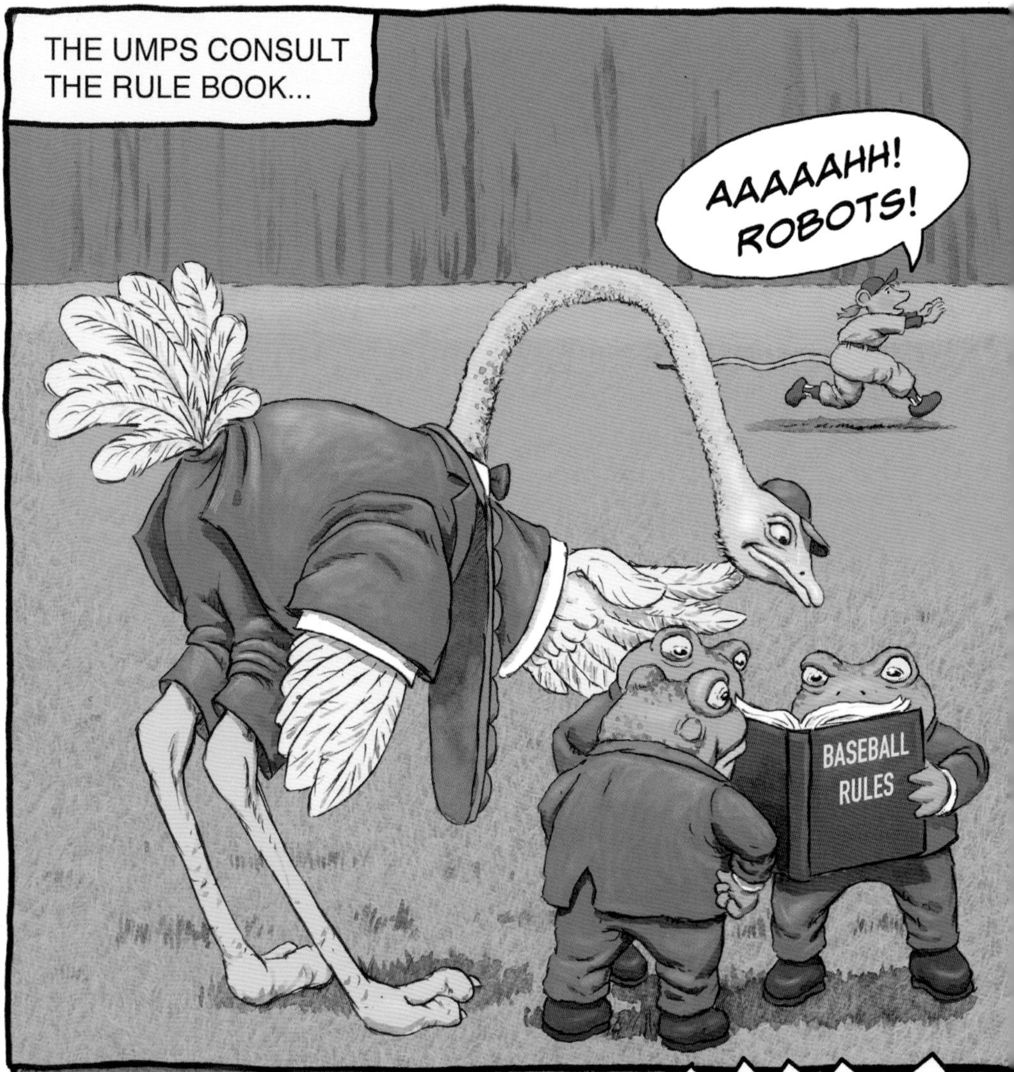
THE UMPS CONSULT THE RULE BOOK...
AAAAAHH! ROBOTS!
BASEBALL RULES

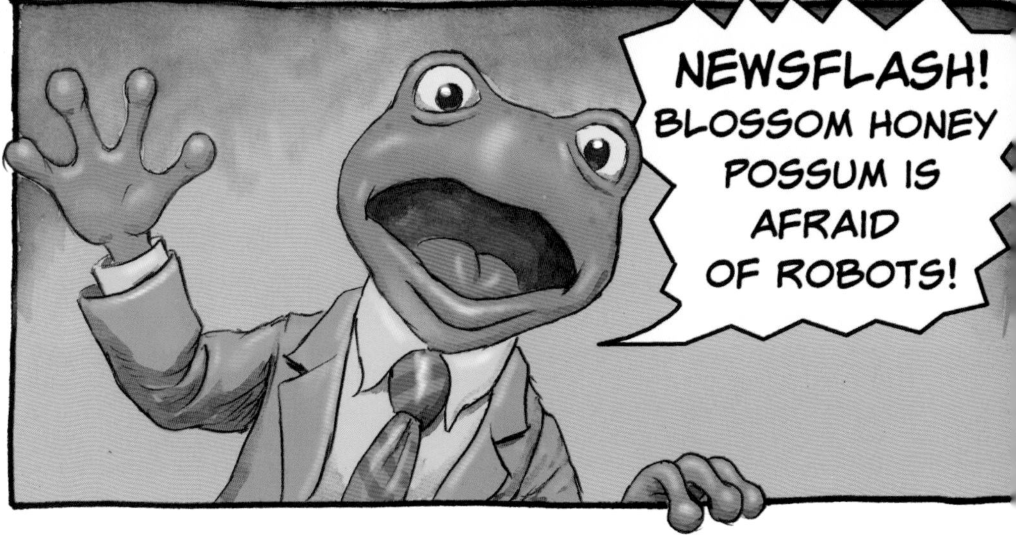
NEWSFLASH! BLOSSOM HONEY POSSUM IS AFRAID OF ROBOTS!

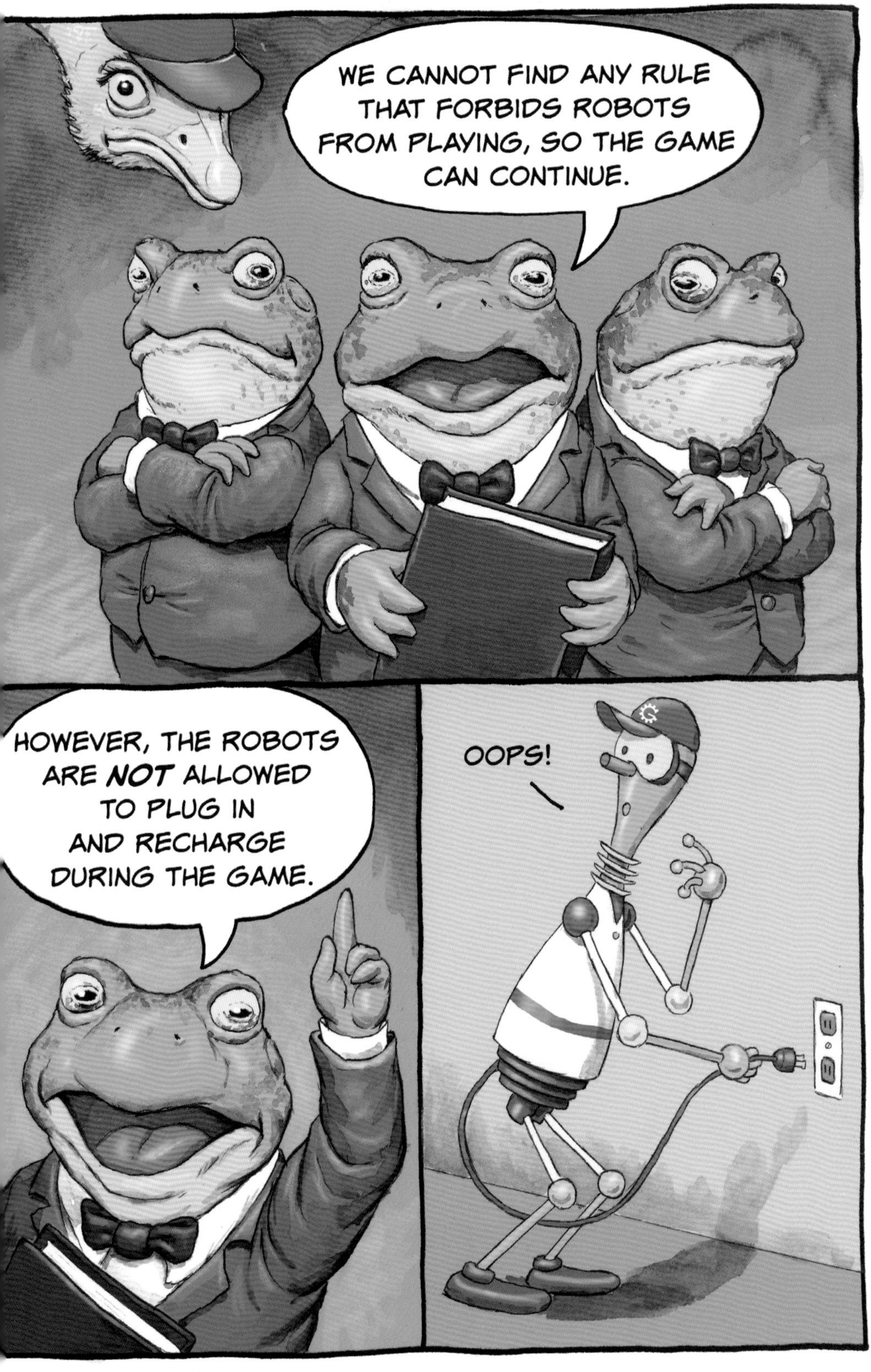
WE CANNOT FIND ANY RULE THAT FORBIDS ROBOTS FROM PLAYING, SO THE GAME CAN CONTINUE.
HOWEVER, THE ROBOTS ARE NOT ALLOWED TO PLUG IN AND RECHARGE DURING THE GAME.
OOPS!

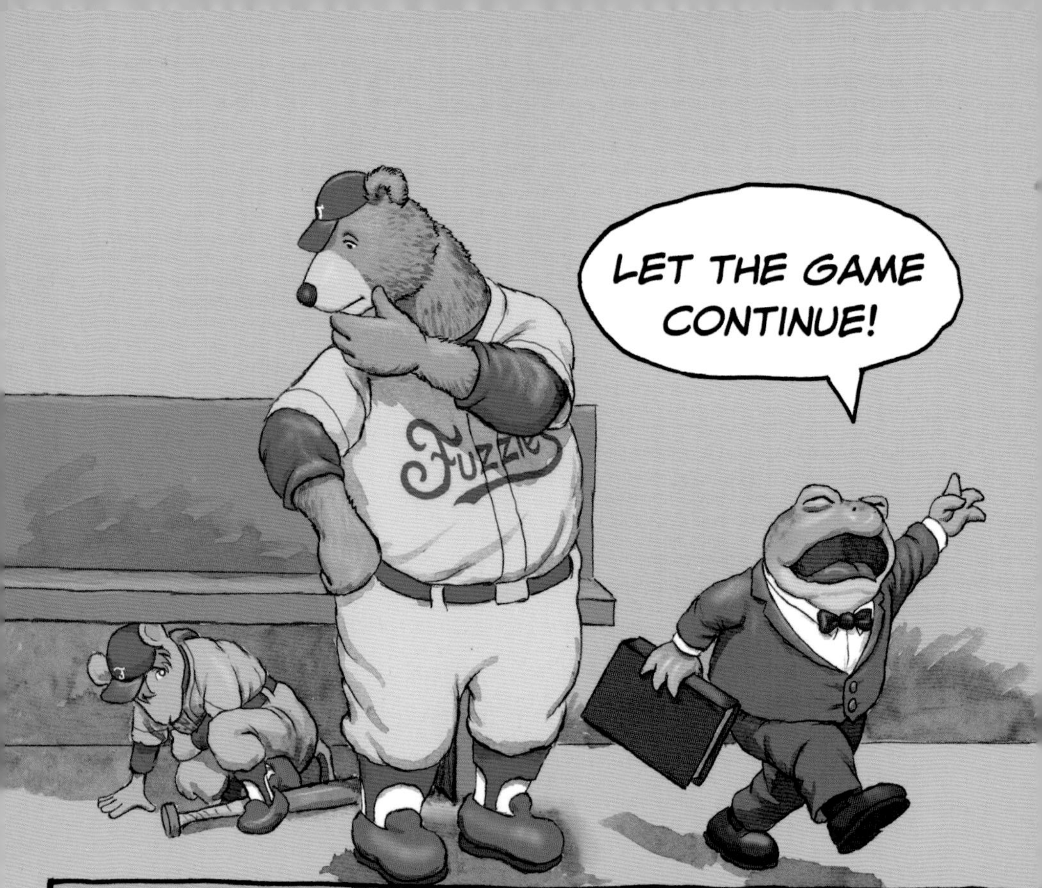
LET THE GAME CONTINUE!

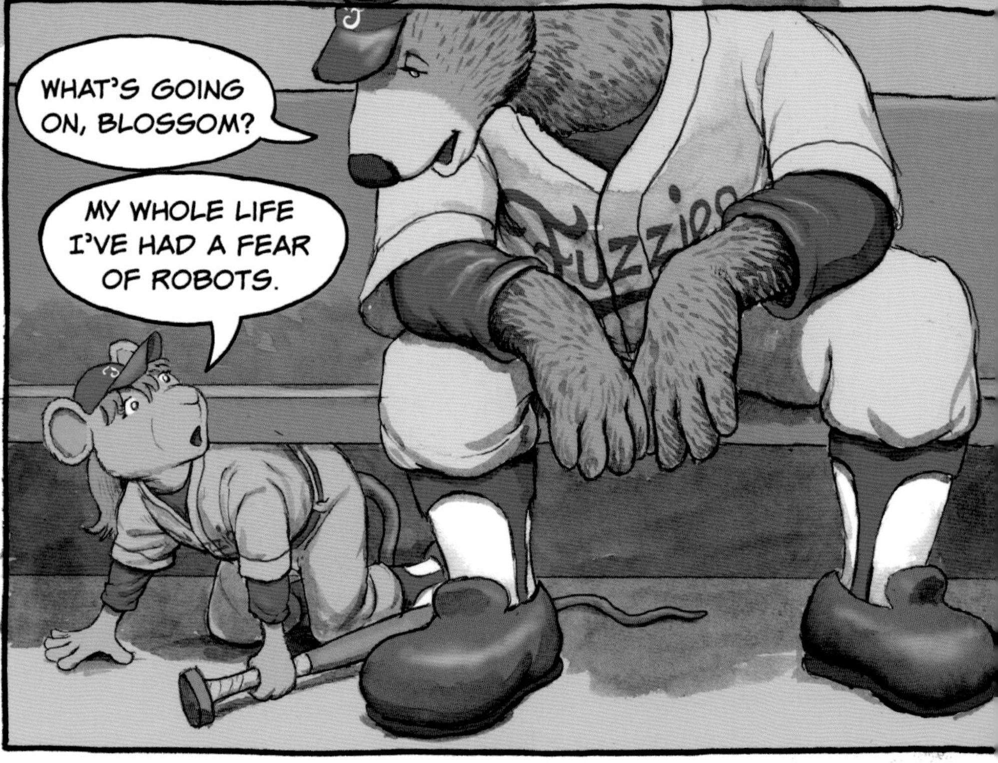
WHAT'S GOING ON, BLOSSOM?
MY WHOLE LIFE I'VE HAD A FEAR OF ROBOTS.

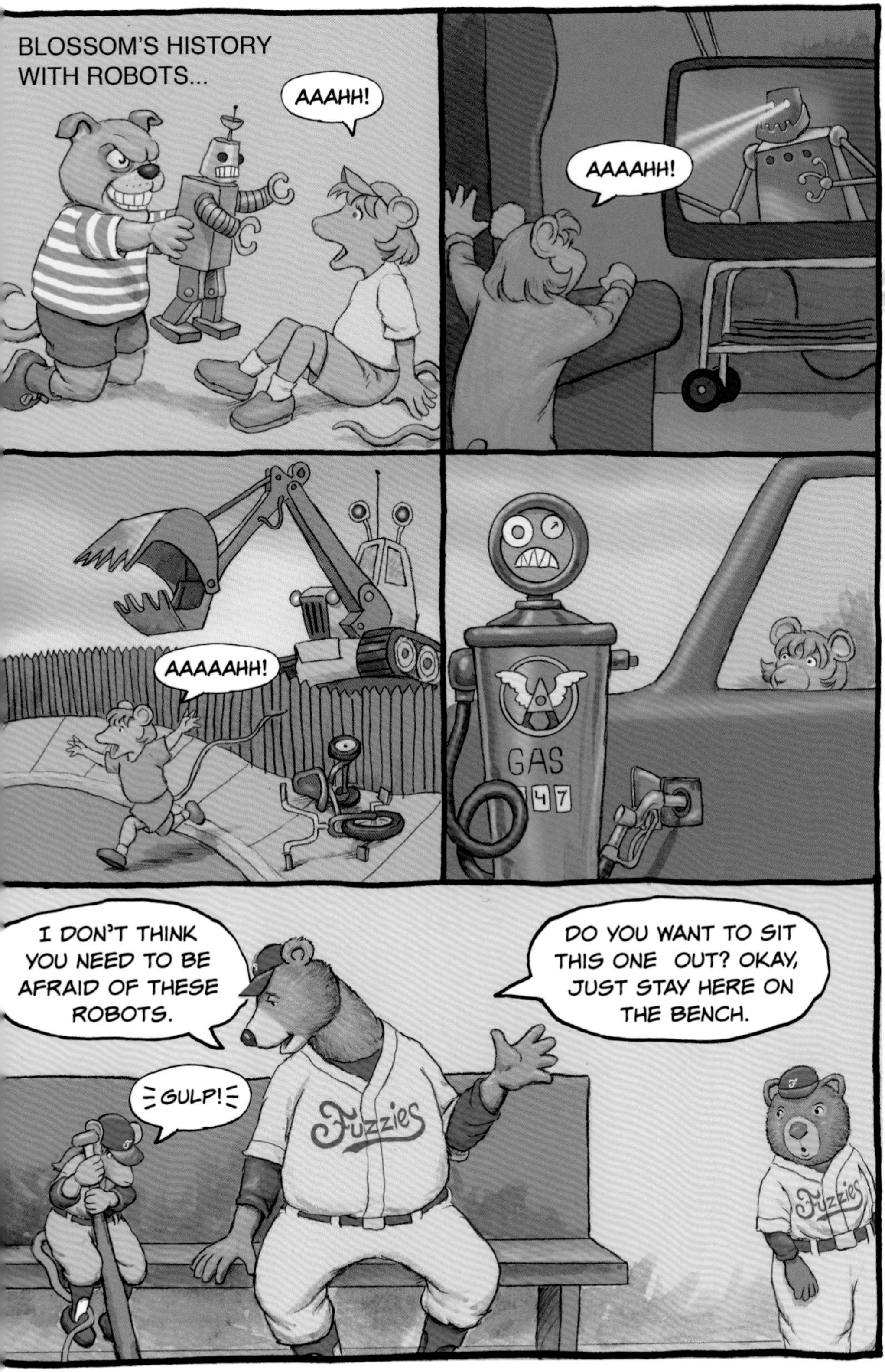
BLOSSOM'S HISTORY WITH ROBOTS...
AAAHH!
AAAAHH!
AAAAAHH!
GAS
47
I DON'T THINK YOU NEED TO BE AFRAID OF THESE ROBOTS.
GULP!
DO YOU WANT TO SIT THIS ONE OUT? OKAY, JUST STAY HERE ON THE BENCH.
Fuzzies
Fuzzies

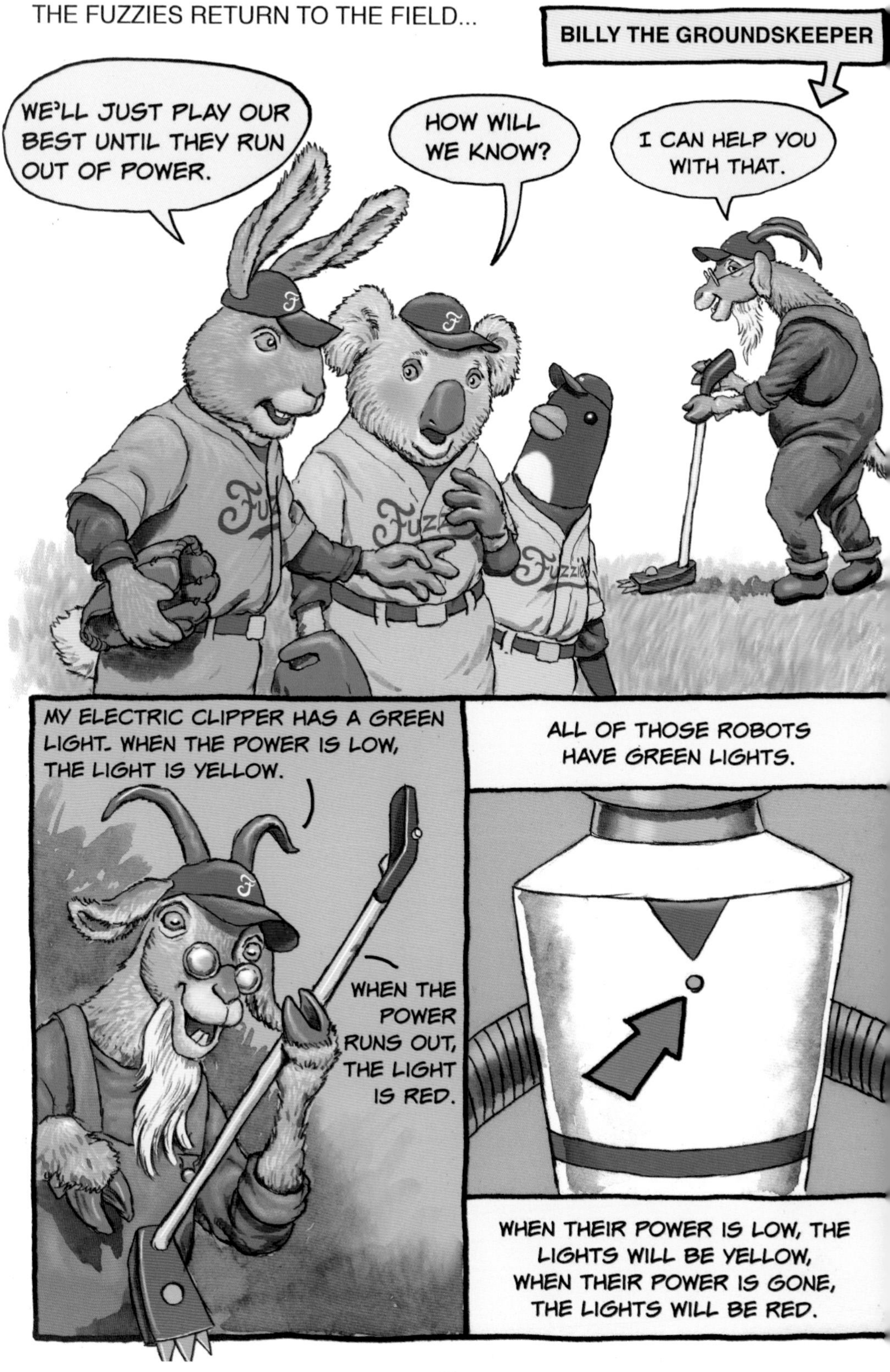
THE FUZZIES RETURN TO THE FIELD...
BILLY THE GROUNDSKEEPER
WE'LL JUST PLAY OUR BEST UNTIL THEY RUN OUT OF POWER.
HOW WILL WE KNOW?
I CAN HELP YOU WITH THAT.
MY ELECTRIC CLIPPER HAS A GREEN LIGHT. WHEN THE POWER IS LOW, THE LIGHT IS YELLOW.
WHEN THE POWER RUNS OUT, THE LIGHT IS RED.
ALL OF THOSE ROBOTS HAVE GREEN LIGHTS.
WHEN THEIR POWER IS LOW, THE LIGHTS WILL BE YELLOW, WHEN THEIR POWER IS GONE, THE LIGHTS WILL BE RED.

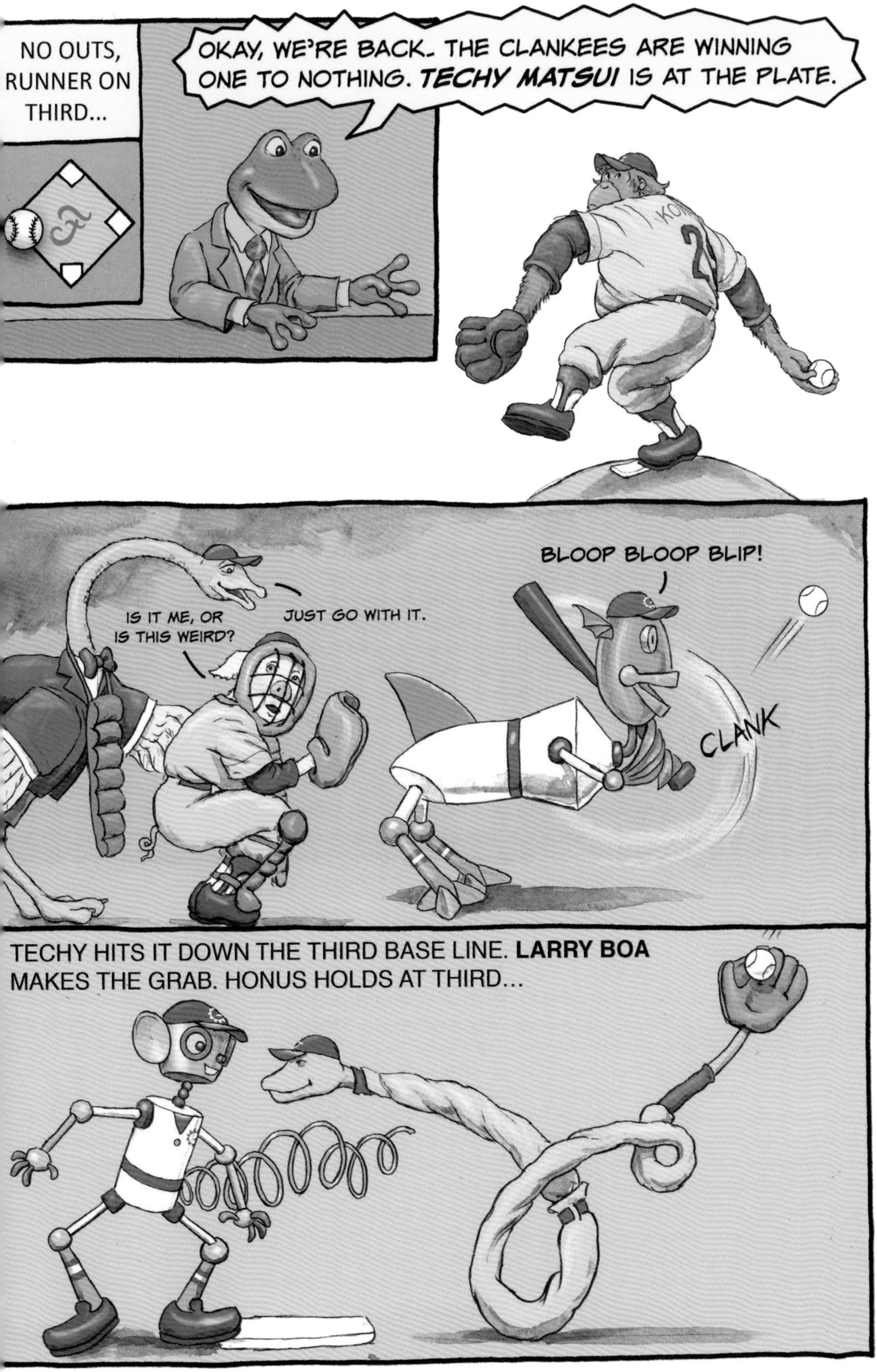
NO OUTS, RUNNER ON THIRD...
OKAY, WE'RE BACK. THE CLANKEES ARE WINNING ONE TO NOTHING. TECHY MATSUI IS AT THE PLATE.
IS IT ME, OR IS THIS WEIRD?
JUST GO WITH IT.
BLOOP BLOOP BLIP!
CLANK
TECHY HITS IT DOWN THE THIRD BASE LINE. LARRY BOA MAKES THE GRAB. HONUS HOLDS AT THIRD...

ONE OUT, RUNNER AT THIRD... THE NEXT BATTER IS *JOHNNY WRENCH*.

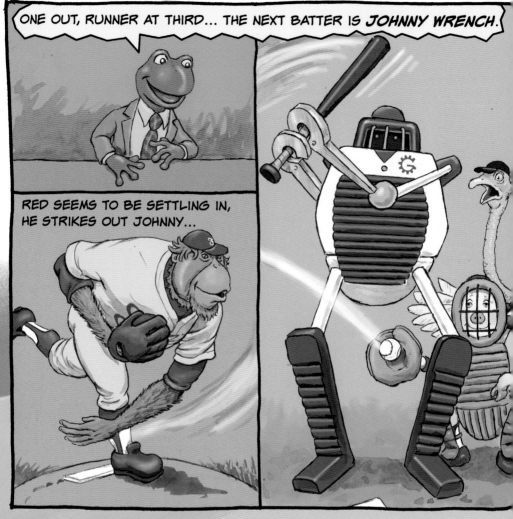

RED SEEMS TO BE SETTLING IN, HE STRIKES OUT JOHNNY...

HONUS IS TAKING A HUGE LEAD AT THIRD.

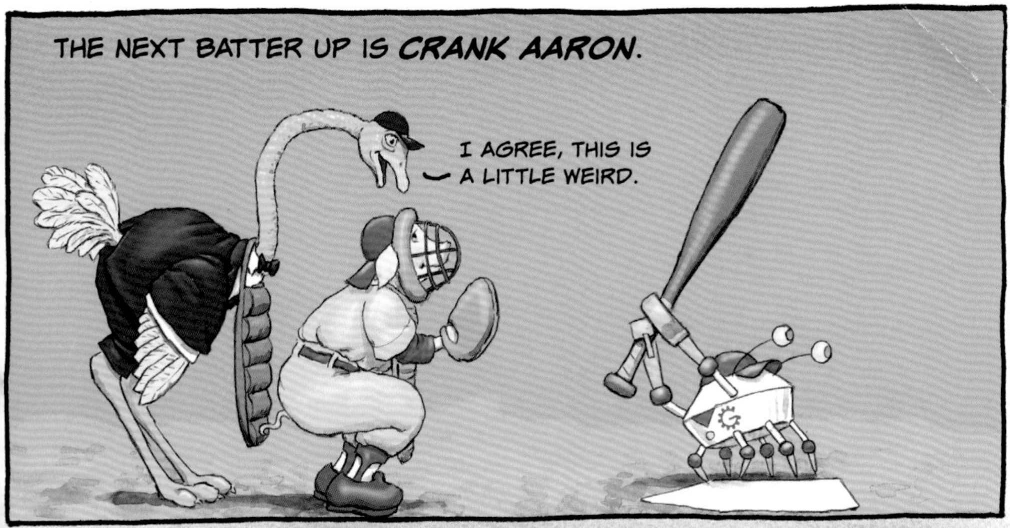
THE NEXT BATTER UP IS CRANK AARON.
I AGREE, THIS IS A LITTLE WEIRD.

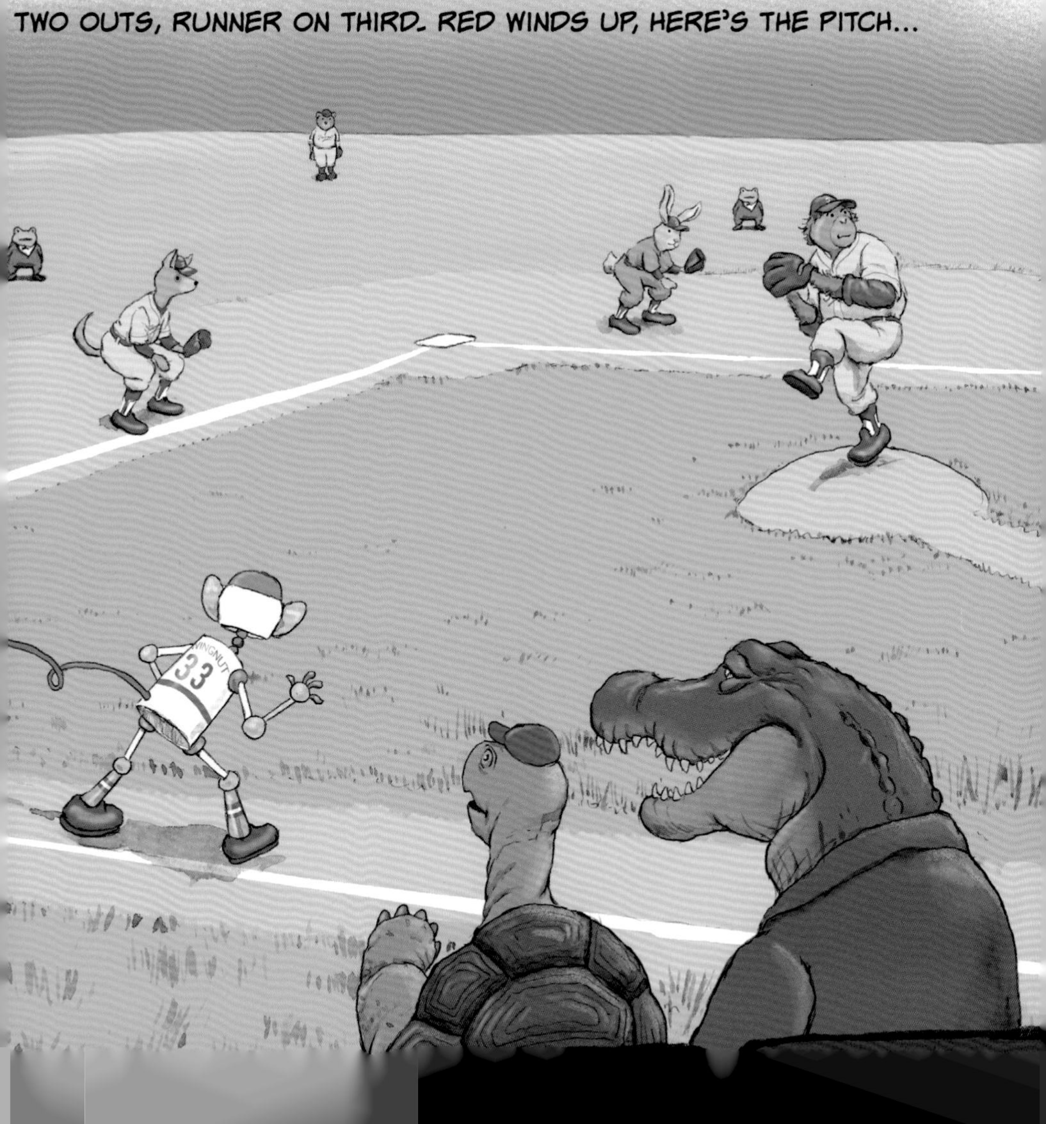
TWO OUTS, RUNNER ON THIRD. RED WINDS UP, HERE'S THE PITCH...
WINGNUT
33

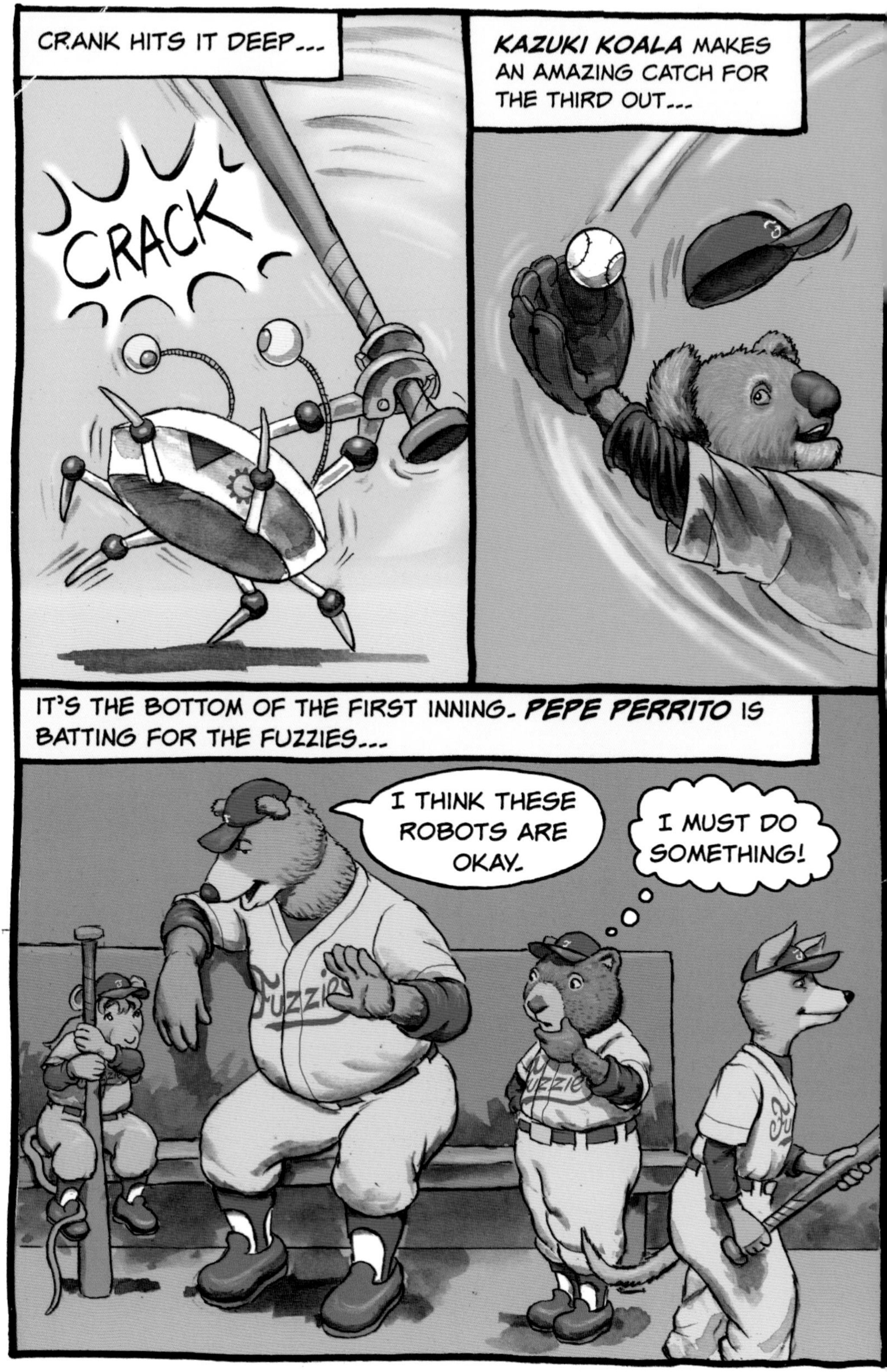
CRANK HITS IT DEEP...
CRACK
KAZUKI KOALA MAKES AN AMAZING CATCH FOR THE THIRD OUT...
IT'S THE BOTTOM OF THE FIRST INNING. PEPE PERRITO IS BATTING FOR THE FUZZIES...
I THINK THESE ROBOTS ARE OKAY.
I MUST DO SOMETHING!

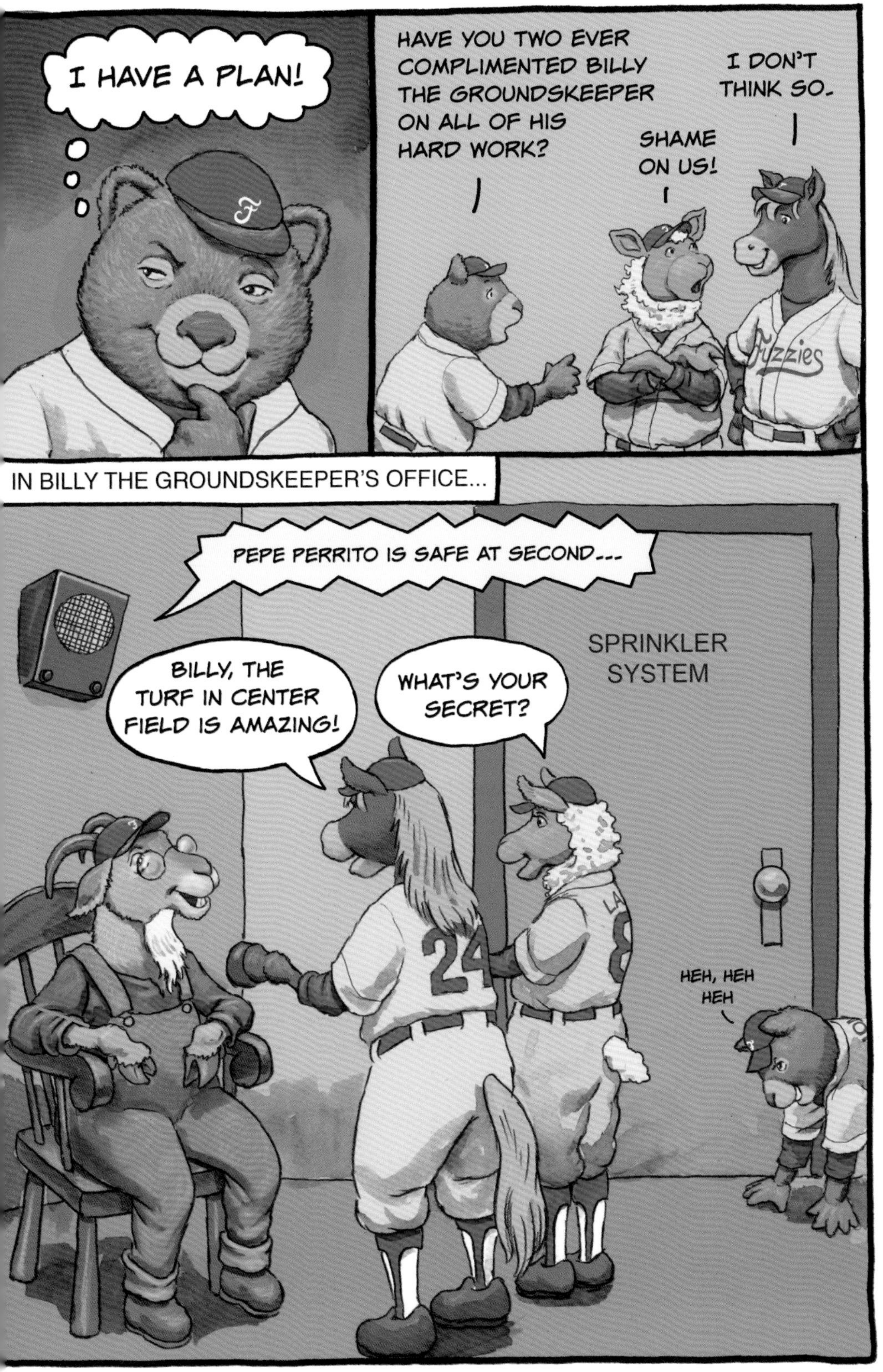
I HAVE A PLAN!
HAVE YOU TWO EVER COMPLIMENTED BILLY THE GROUNDSKEEPER ON ALL OF HIS HARD WORK?
SHAME ON US!
I DON'T THINK SO.
IN BILLY THE GROUNDSKEEPER'S OFFICE...
PEPE PERRITO IS SAFE AT SECOND...
SPRINKLER SYSTEM
BILLY, THE TURF IN CENTER FIELD IS AMAZING!
WHAT'S YOUR SECRET?
HEH, HEH HEH

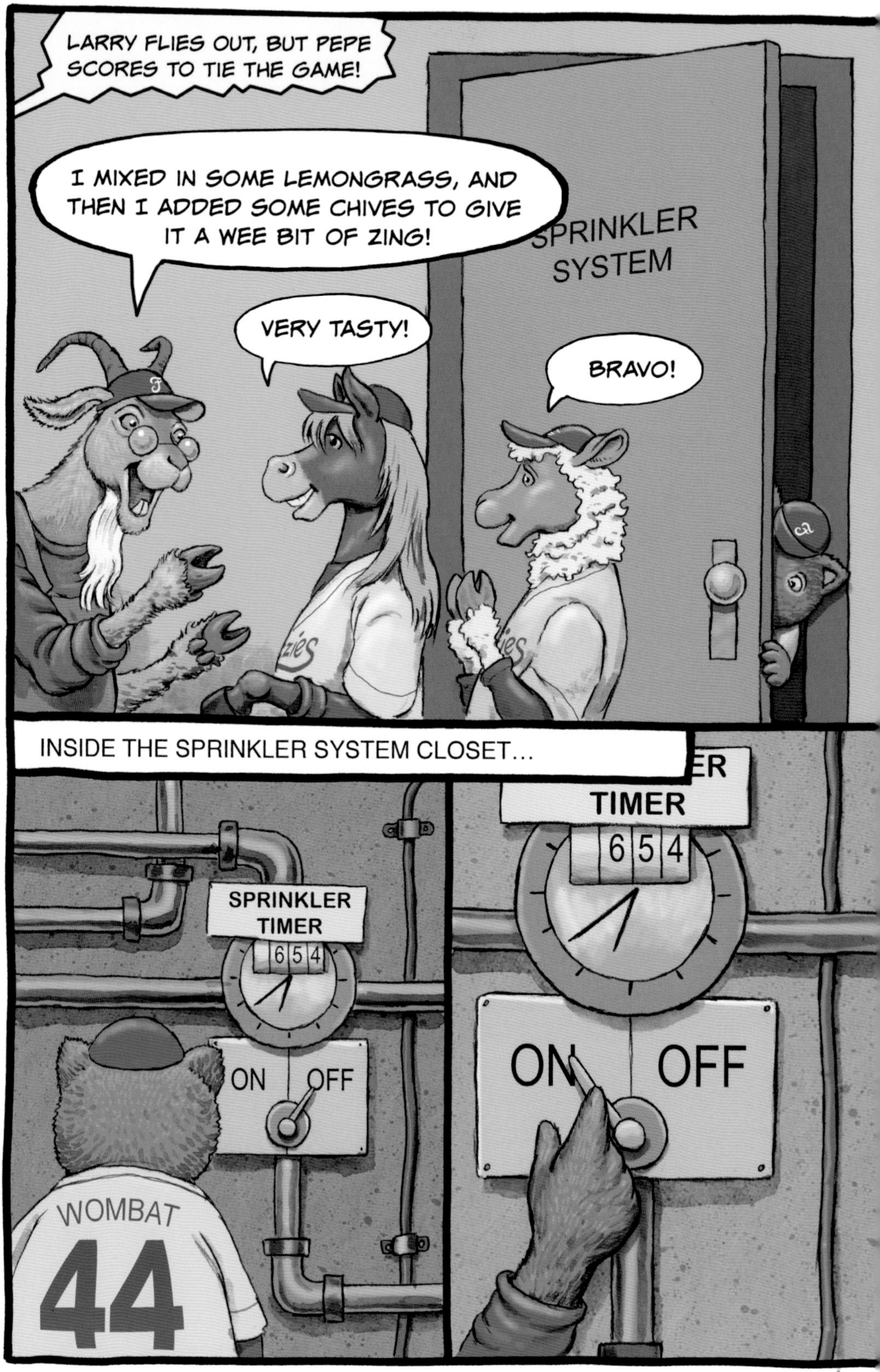
LARRY FLIES OUT, BUT PEPE SCORES TO TIE THE GAME!
I MIXED IN SOME LEMONGRASS, AND THEN I ADDED SOME CHIVES TO GIVE IT A WEE BIT OF ZING!
SPRINKLER SYSTEM
VERY TASTY!
BRAVO!
INSIDE THE SPRINKLER SYSTEM CLOSET…
SPRINKLER TIMER
654
ON
OFF
WOMBAT
44
TIMER
654
ON
OFF

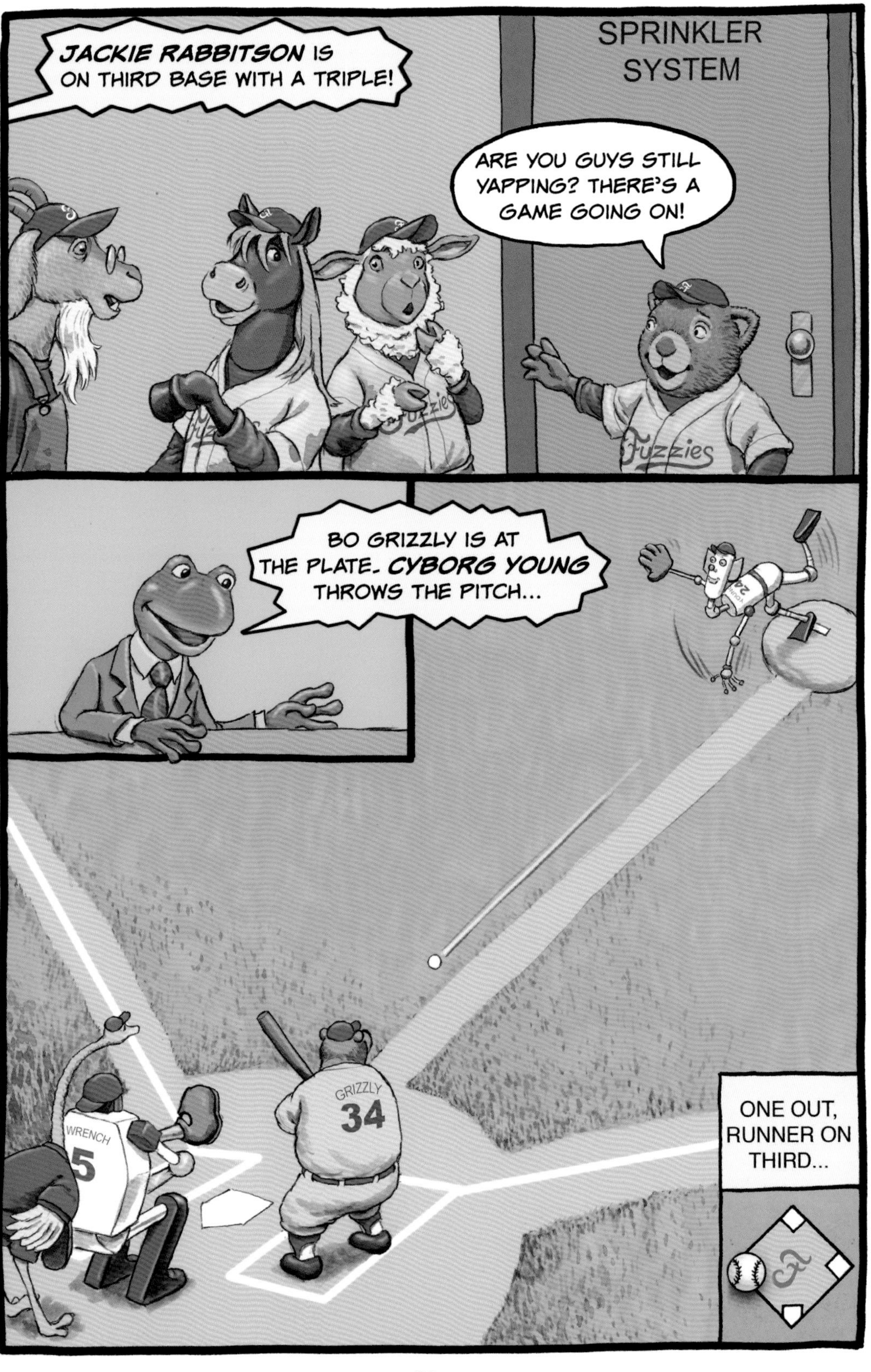
JACKIE RABBITSON IS ON THIRD BASE WITH A TRIPLE!
SPRINKLER SYSTEM
ARE YOU GUYS STILL YAPPING? THERE'S A GAME GOING ON!
Fuzzies
BO GRIZZLY IS AT THE PLATE. CYBORG YOUNG THROWS THE PITCH...
GRIZZLY
34
WRENCH
5
ONE OUT, RUNNER ON THIRD...

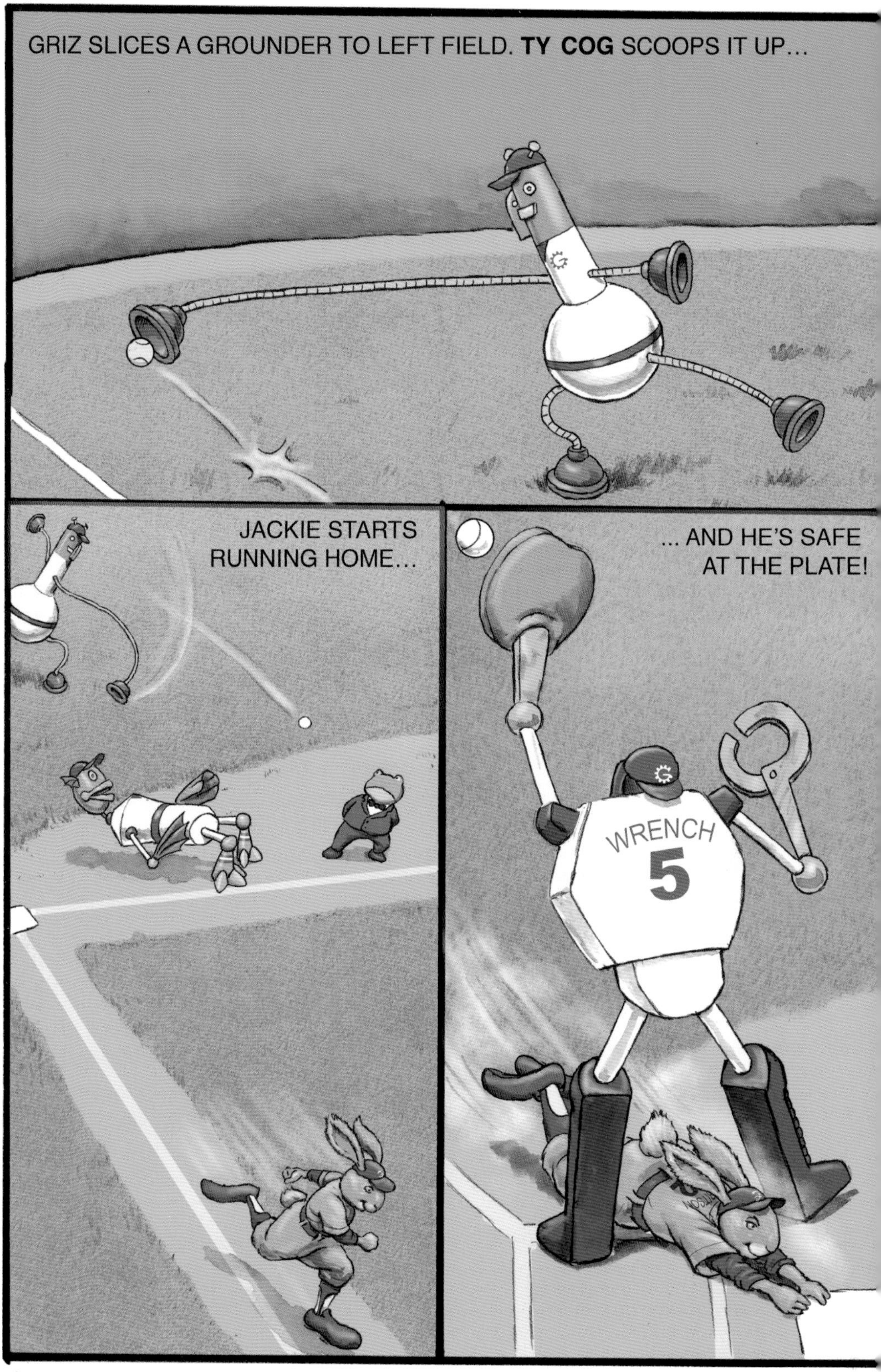
GRIZ SLICES A GROUNDER TO LEFT FIELD. **TY COG** SCOOPS IT UP...
JACKIE STARTS RUNNING HOME...
... AND HE'S SAFE AT THE PLATE!
WRENCH
5

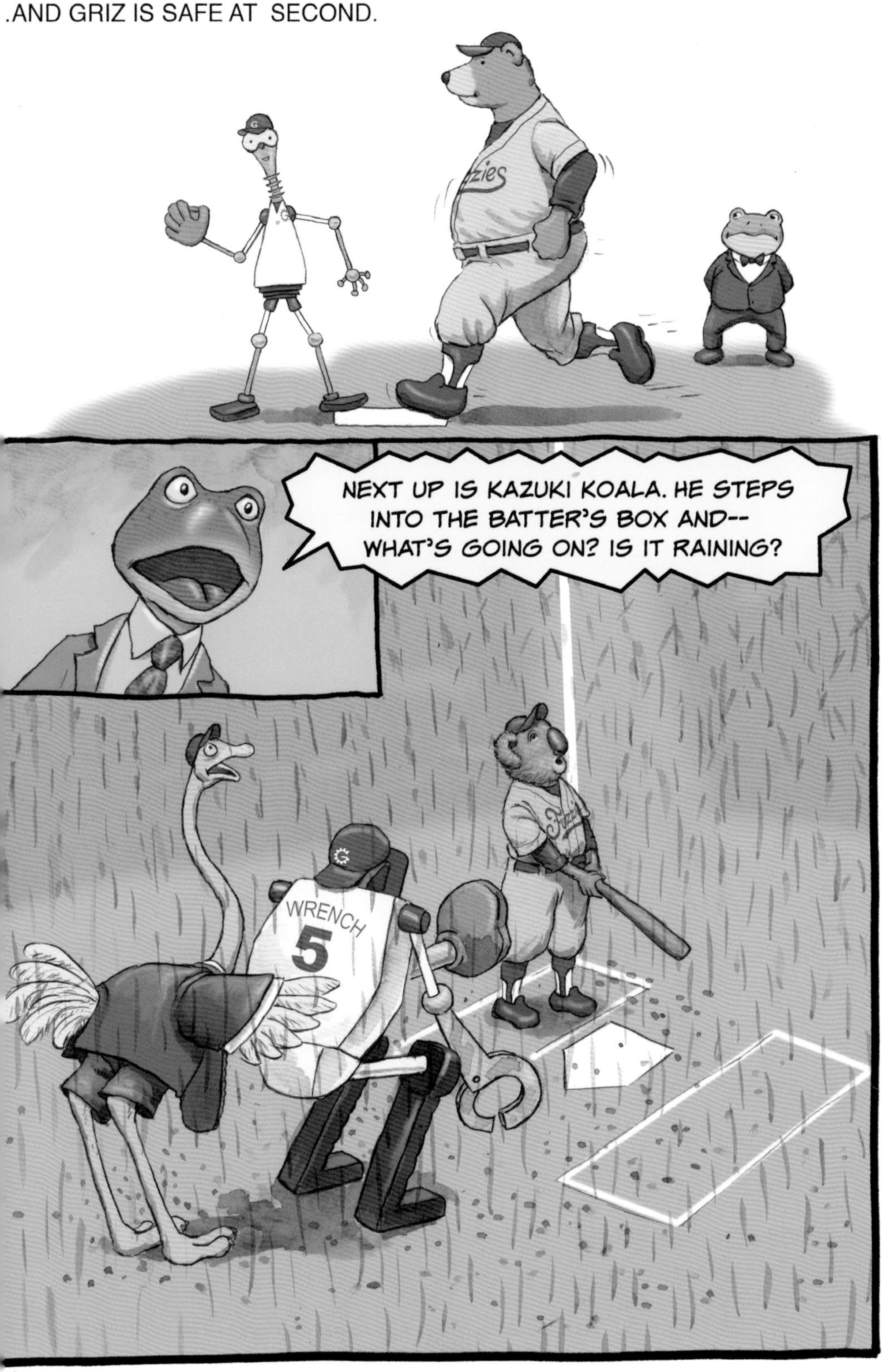
.AND GRIZ IS SAFE AT SECOND.
NEXT UP IS KAZUKI KOALA. HE STEPS INTO THE BATTER'S BOX AND-- WHAT'S GOING ON? IS IT RAINING?
WRENCH
5

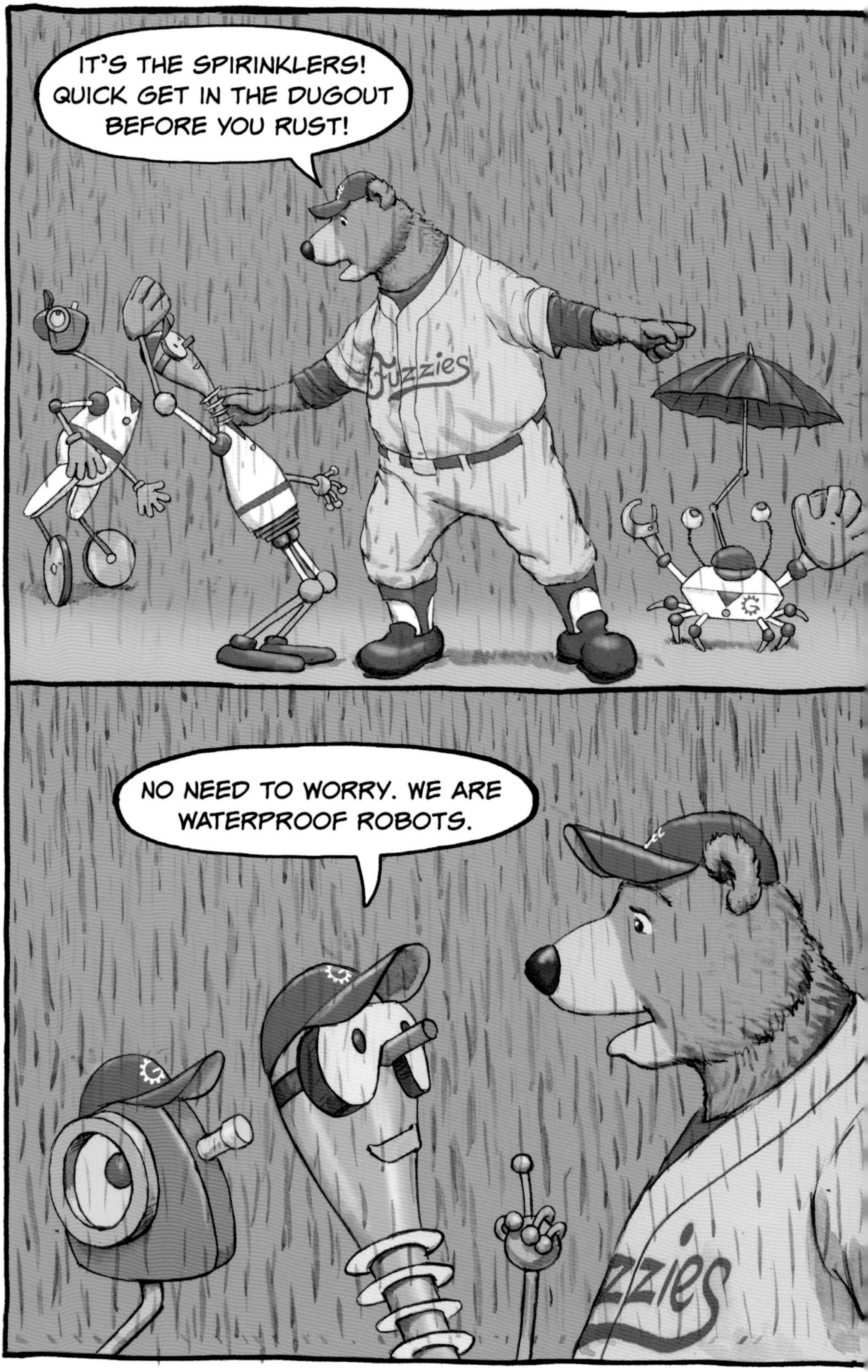
IT'S THE SPIRINKLERS! QUICK GET IN THE DUGOUT BEFORE YOU RUST!
Fuzzies
NO NEED TO WORRY. WE ARE WATERPROOF ROBOTS.

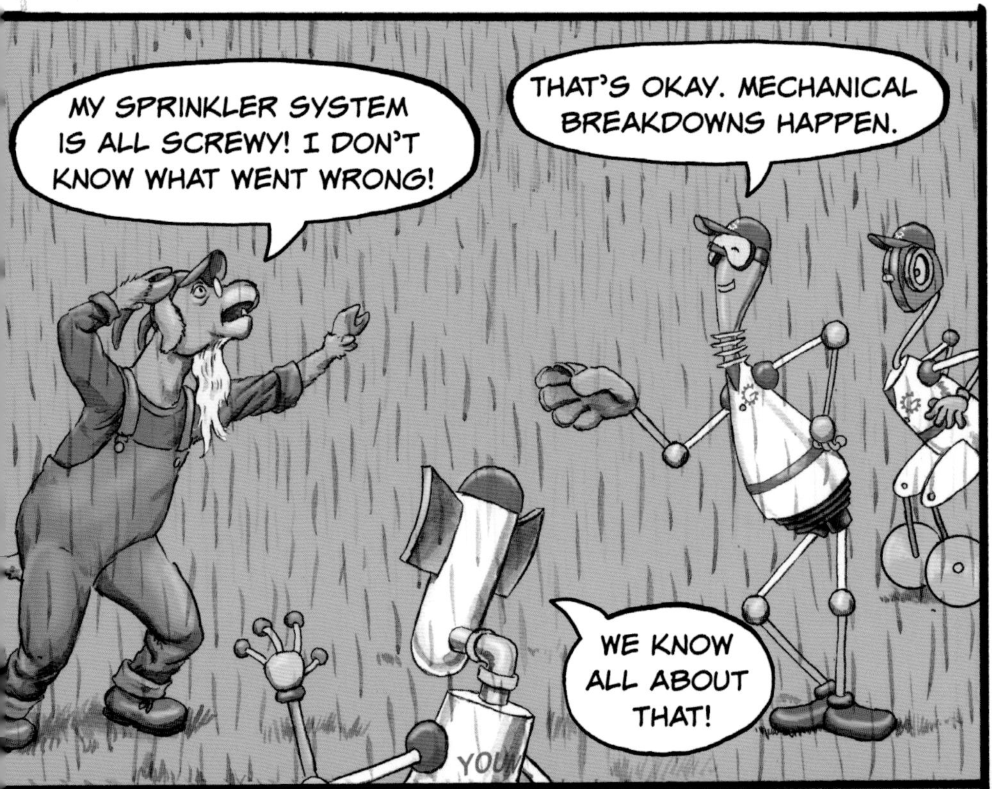
MY SPRINKLER SYSTEM IS ALL SCREWY! I DON'T KNOW WHAT WENT WRONG!
THAT'S OKAY. MECHANICAL BREAKDOWNS HAPPEN.
WE KNOW ALL ABOUT THAT!
YOU
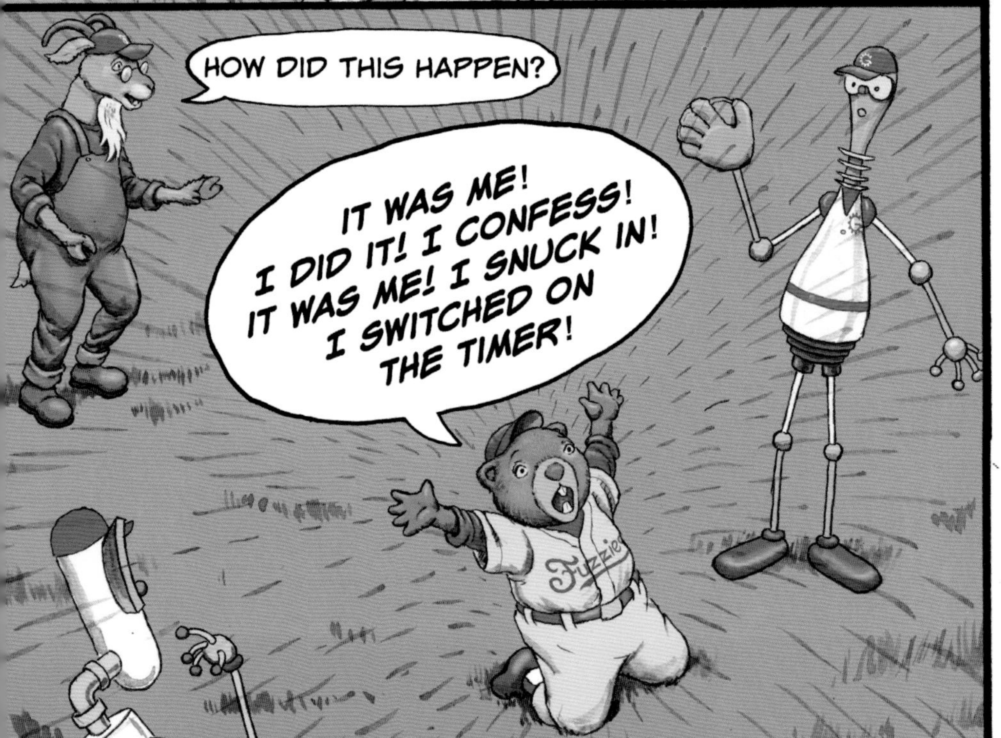
HOW DID THIS HAPPEN?
IT WAS ME! I DID IT! I CONFESS! IT WAS ME! I SNUCK IN! I SWITCHED ON THE TIMER!
Fuzzies
OUNG

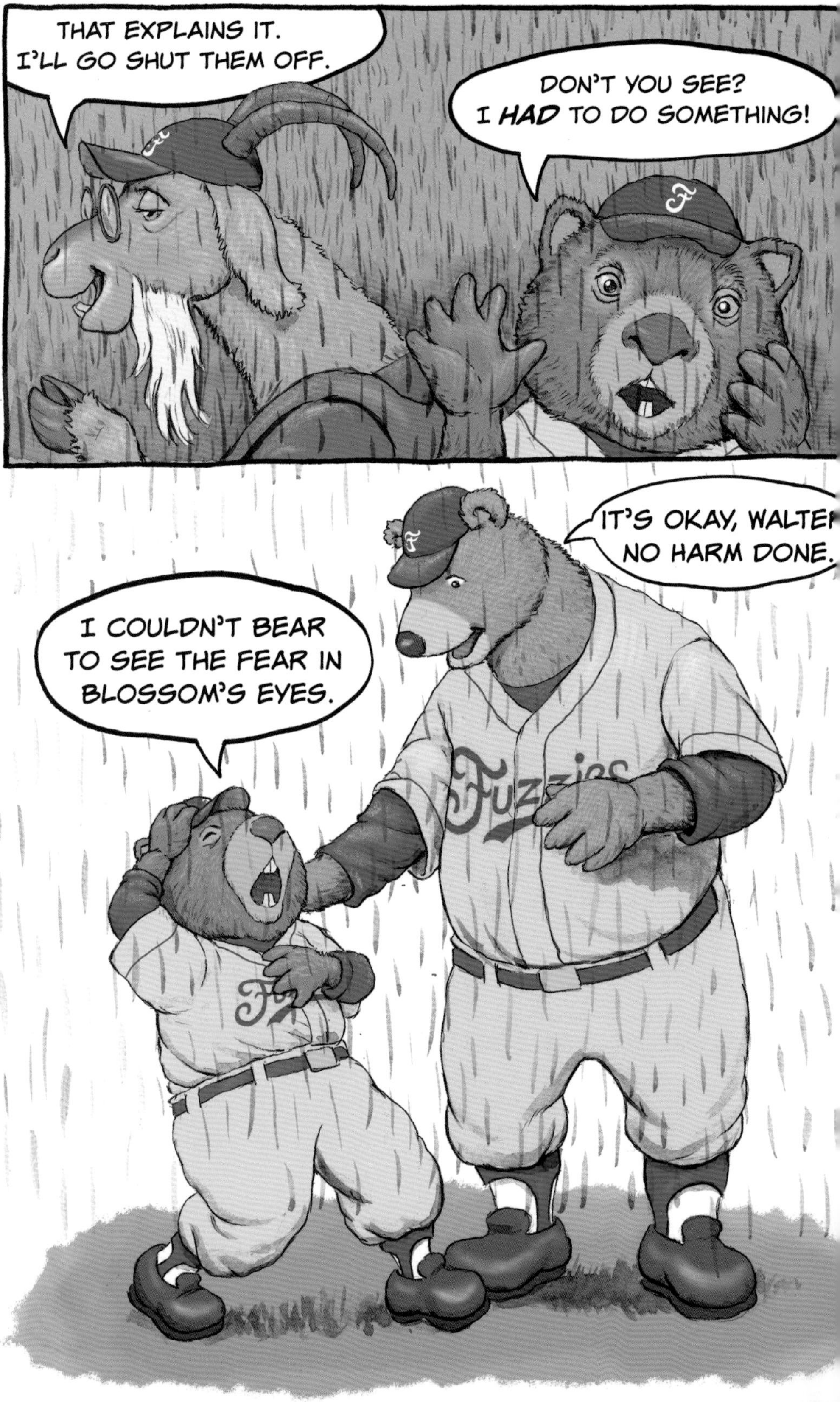
THAT EXPLAINS IT. I'LL GO SHUT THEM OFF.
DON'T YOU SEE? I *HAD* TO DO SOMETHING!
IT'S OKAY, WALTE
NO HARM DONE.
I COULDN'T BEAR TO SEE THE FEAR IN BLOSSOM'S EYES.
Fuzzies

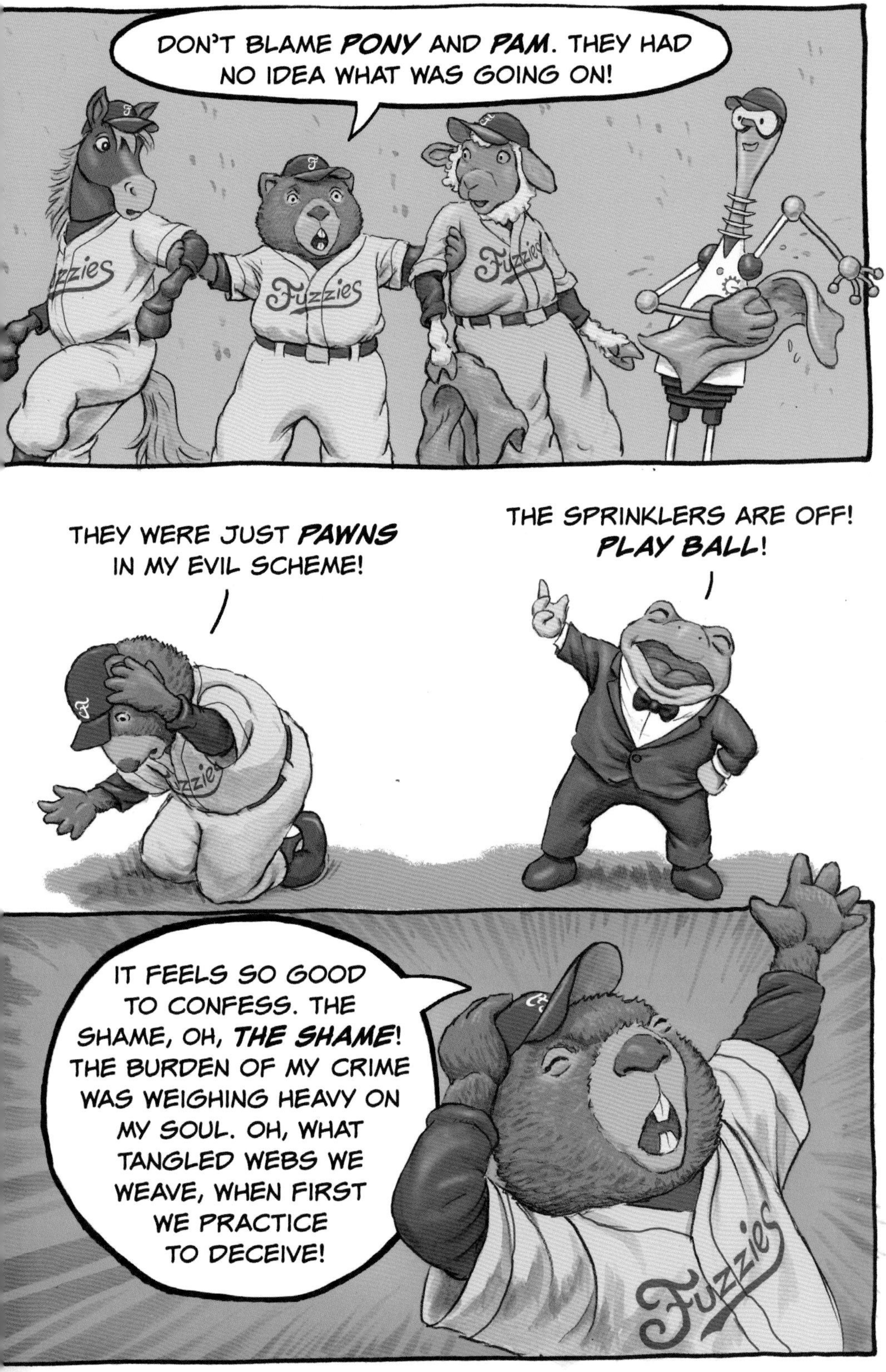
DON'T BLAME PONY AND PAM. THEY HAD NO IDEA WHAT WAS GOING ON!
THEY WERE JUST PAWNS IN MY EVIL SCHEME!
THE SPRINKLERS ARE OFF! PLAY BALL!
IT FEELS SO GOOD TO CONFESS. THE SHAME, OH, THE SHAME! THE BURDEN OF MY CRIME WAS WEIGHING HEAVY ON MY SOUL. OH, WHAT TANGLED WEBS WE WEAVE, WHEN FIRST WE PRACTICE TO DECEIVE!

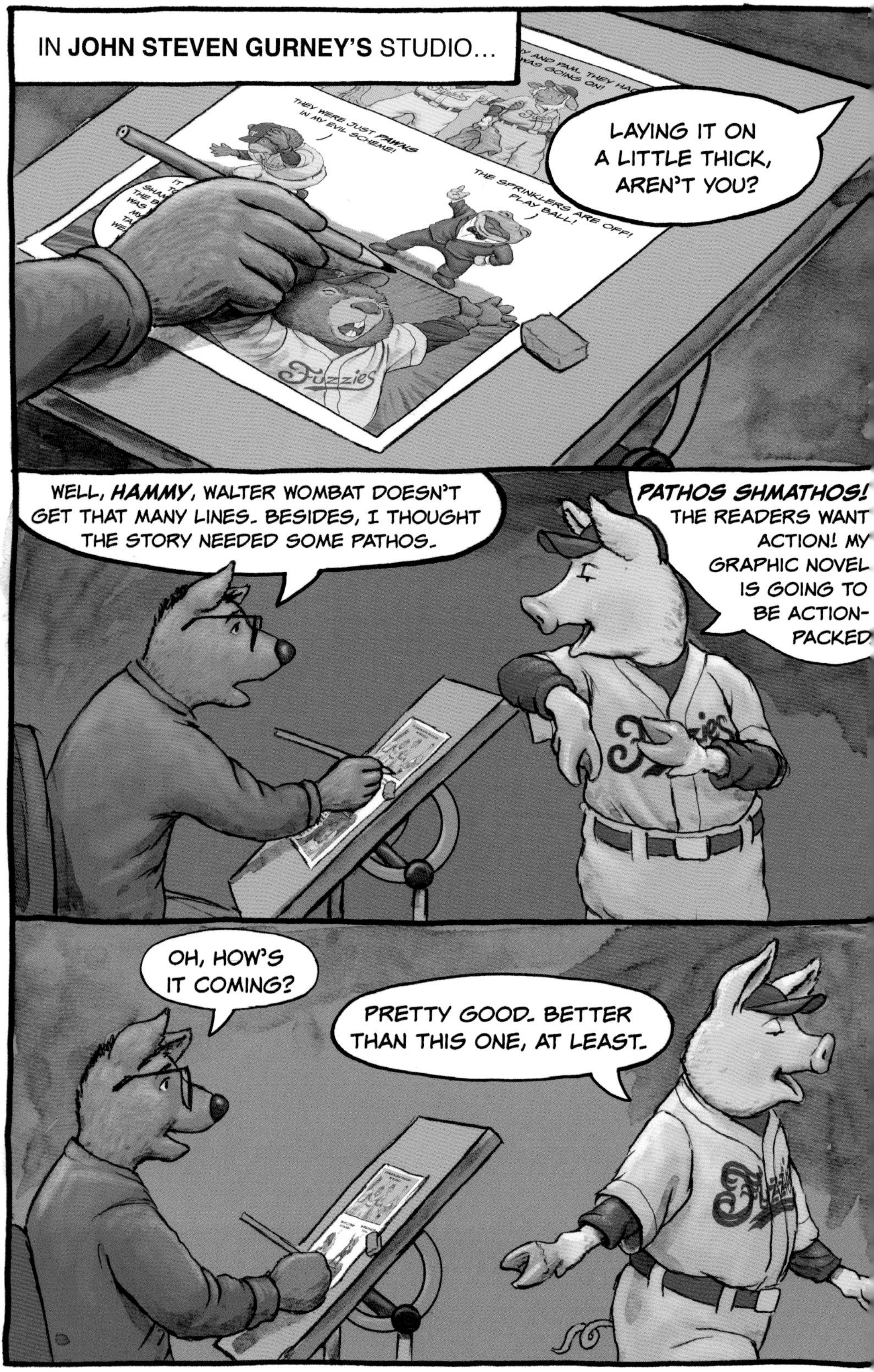
IN JOHN STEVEN GURNEY'S STUDIO...
THEY WERE JUST PAWNS IN MY EVIL SCHEME!
THE SPRINKLERS ARE OFF! PLAY BALL!
Fuzzies
LAYING IT ON A LITTLE THICK, AREN'T YOU?
WELL, HAMMY, WALTER WOMBAT DOESN'T GET THAT MANY LINES. BESIDES, I THOUGHT THE STORY NEEDED SOME PATHOS.
PATHOS SHMATHOS! THE READERS WANT ACTION! MY GRAPHIC NOVEL IS GOING TO BE ACTION-PACKED.
OH, HOW'S IT COMING?
PRETTY GOOD. BETTER THAN THIS ONE, AT LEAST.

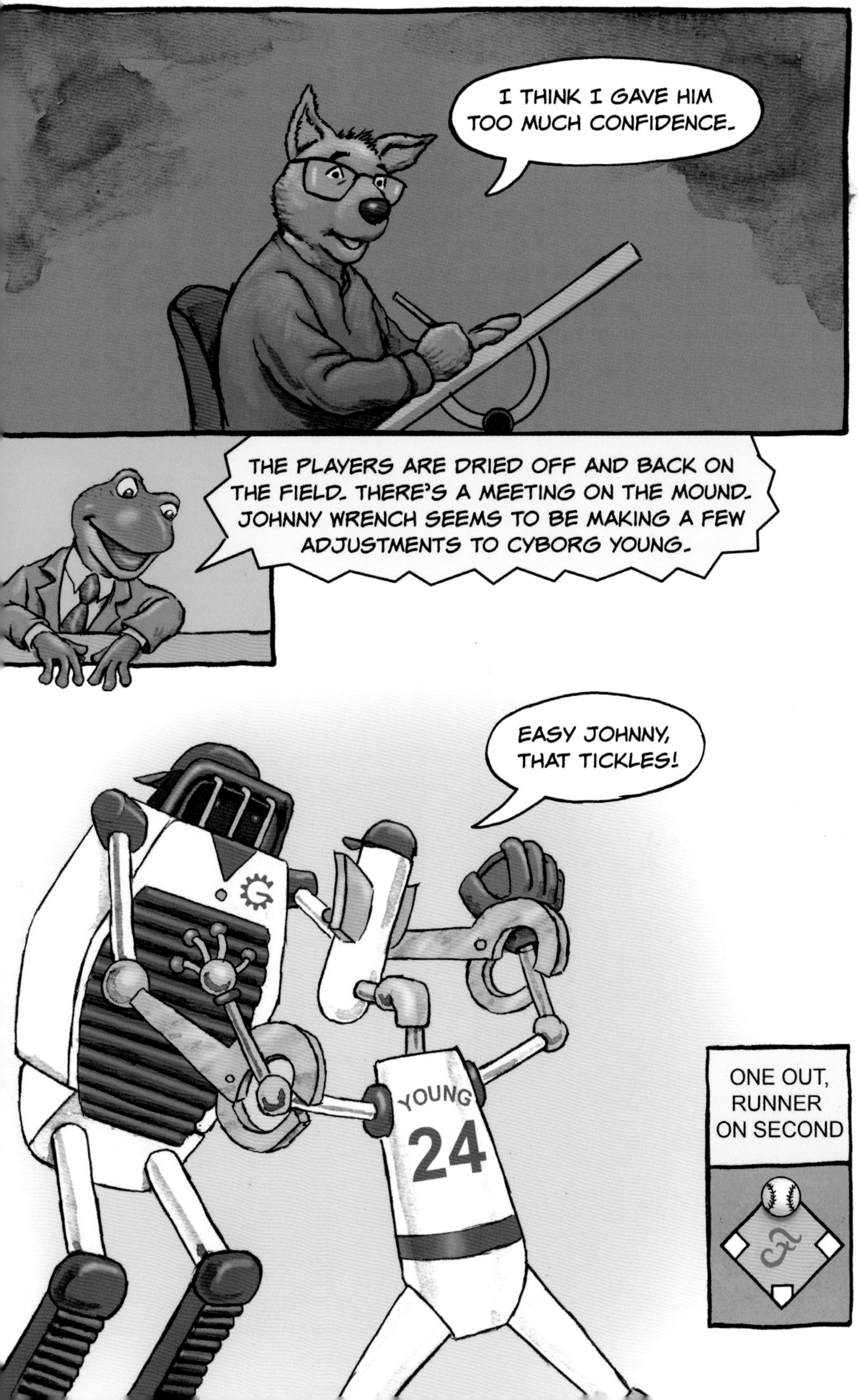
I THINK I GAVE HIM TOO MUCH CONFIDENCE.
THE PLAYERS ARE DRIED OFF AND BACK ON THE FIELD. THERE'S A MEETING ON THE MOUND. JOHNNY WRENCH SEEMS TO BE MAKING A FEW ADJUSTMENTS TO CYBORG YOUNG.
EASY JOHNNY, THAT TICKLES!
YOUNG
24
ONE OUT, RUNNER ON SECOND

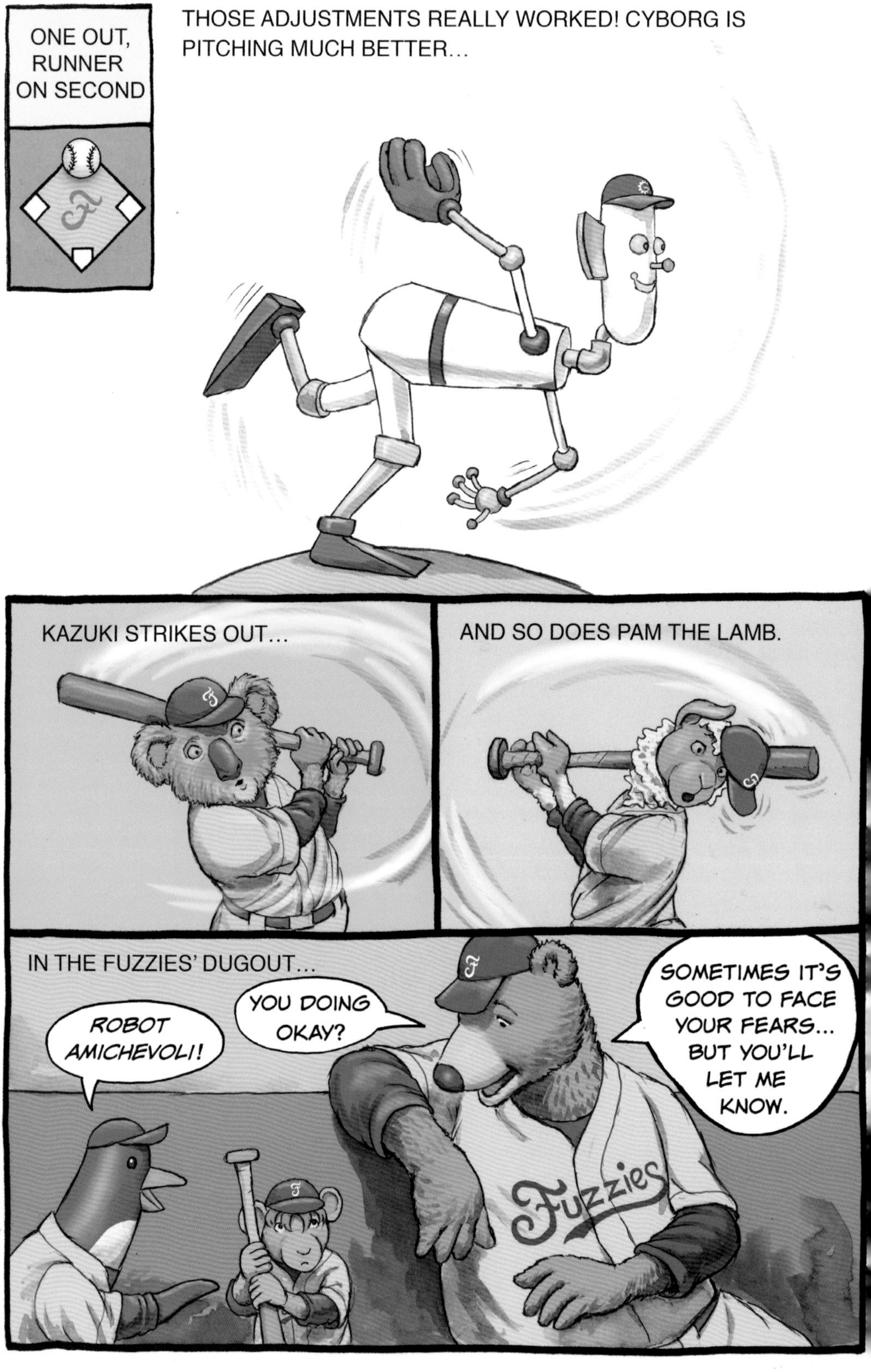
ONE OUT, RUNNER ON SECOND
THOSE ADJUSTMENTS REALLY WORKED! CYBORG IS PITCHING MUCH BETTER…
KAZUKI STRIKES OUT…
AND SO DOES PAM THE LAMB.
IN THE FUZZIES' DUGOUT…
ROBOT AMICHEVOLI!
YOU DOING OKAY?
SOMETIMES IT'S GOOD TO FACE YOUR FEARS… BUT YOU'LL LET ME KNOW.
Fuzzies

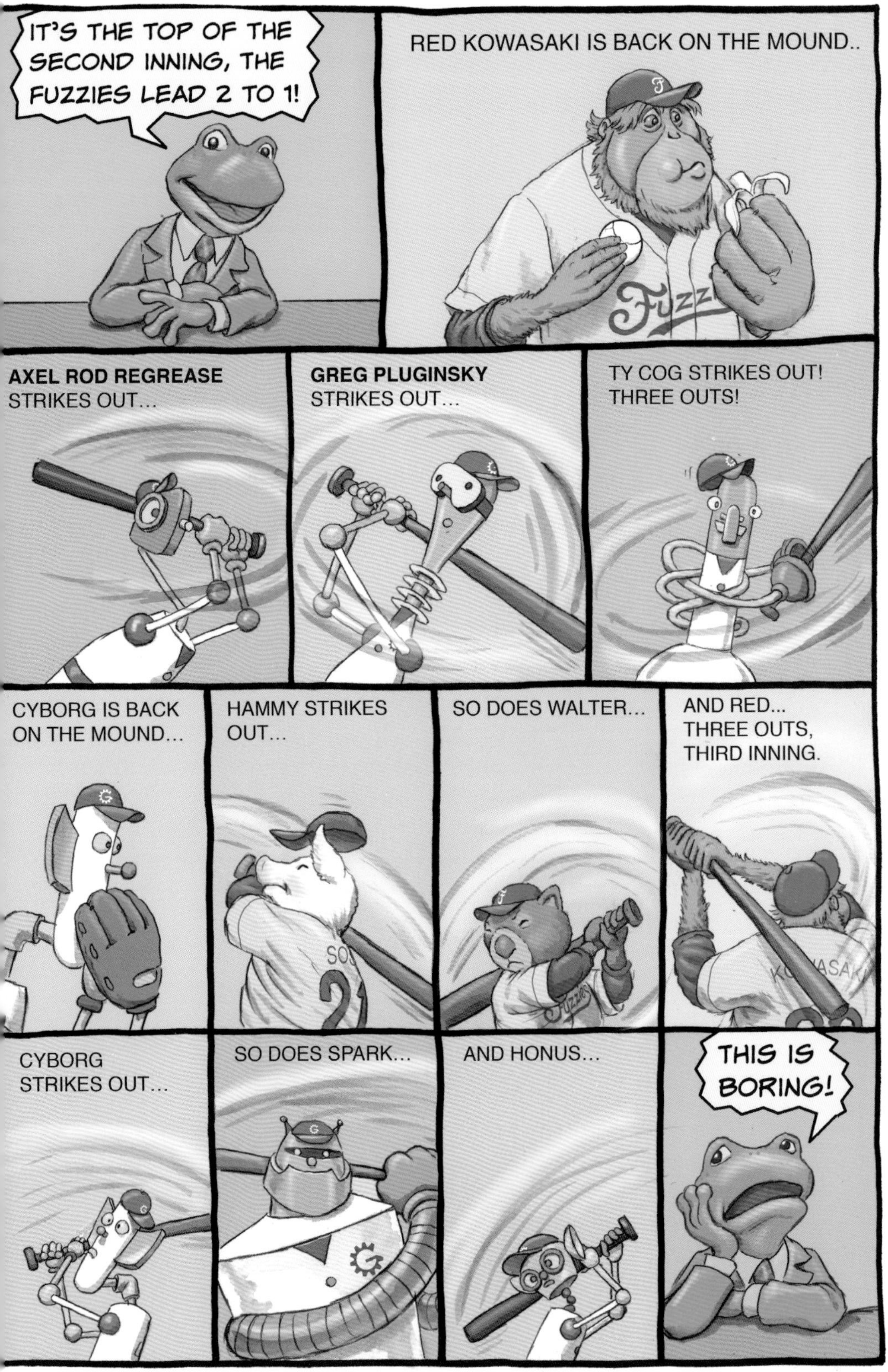
IT'S THE TOP OF THE SECOND INNING, THE FUZZIES LEAD 2 TO 1!
RED KOWASAKI IS BACK ON THE MOUND..
FUZZ
AXEL ROD REGREASE STRIKES OUT...
GREG PLUGINSKY STRIKES OUT...
TY COG STRIKES OUT! THREE OUTS!
CYBORG IS BACK ON THE MOUND...
HAMMY STRIKES OUT...
SO DOES WALTER...
AND RED... THREE OUTS, THIRD INNING.
KOWASAKI
CYBORG STRIKES OUT...
SO DOES SPARK...
AND HONUS...
THIS IS BORING!

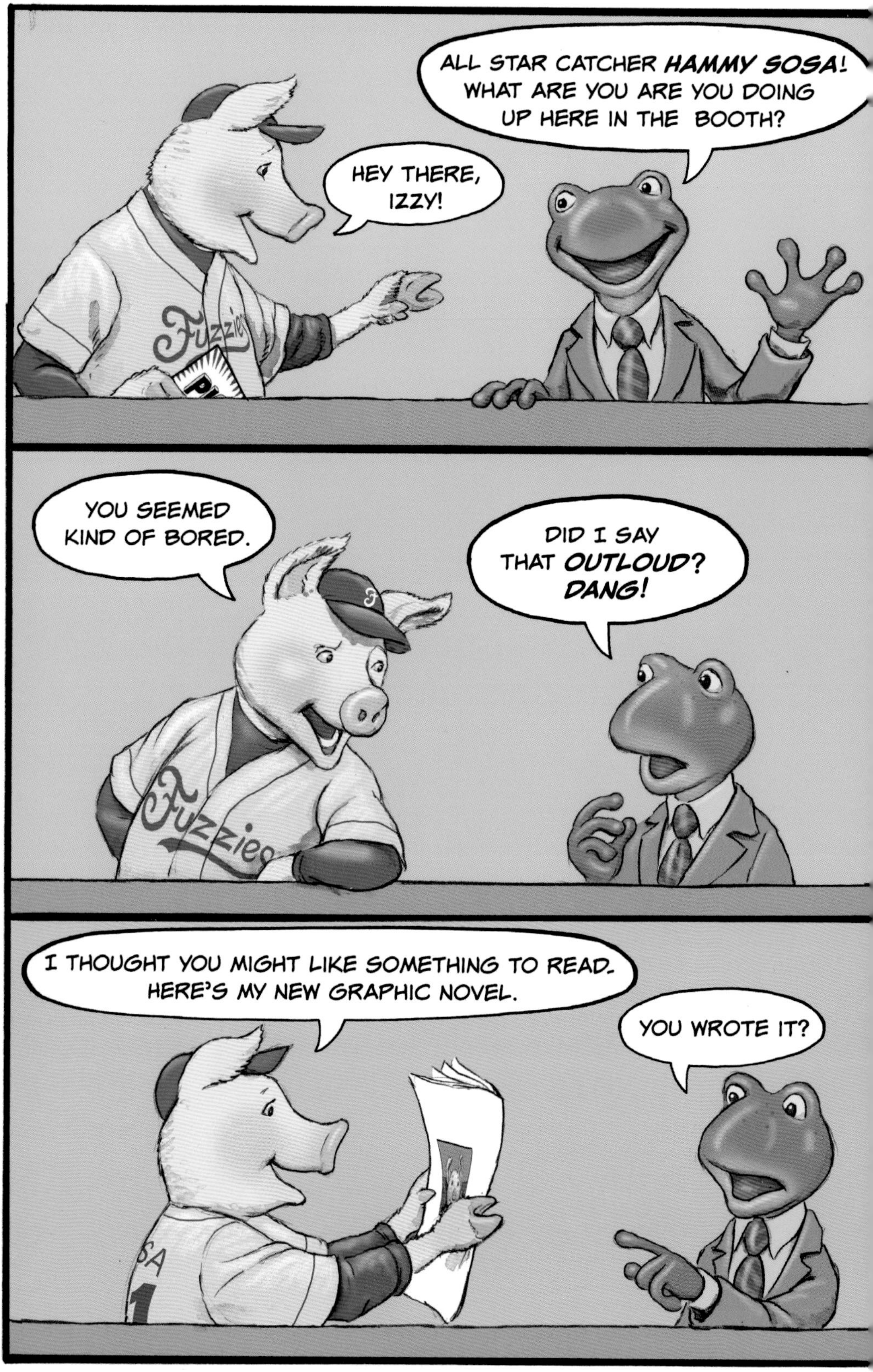
ALL STAR CATCHER **HAMMY SOSA**! WHAT ARE YOU ARE YOU DOING UP HERE IN THE BOOTH?
HEY THERE, IZZY!
Fuzzies
YOU SEEMED KIND OF BORED.
DID I SAY THAT **OUTLOUD**? **DANG**!
Fuzzies
I THOUGHT YOU MIGHT LIKE SOMETHING TO READ. HERE'S MY NEW GRAPHIC NOVEL.
YOU WROTE IT?

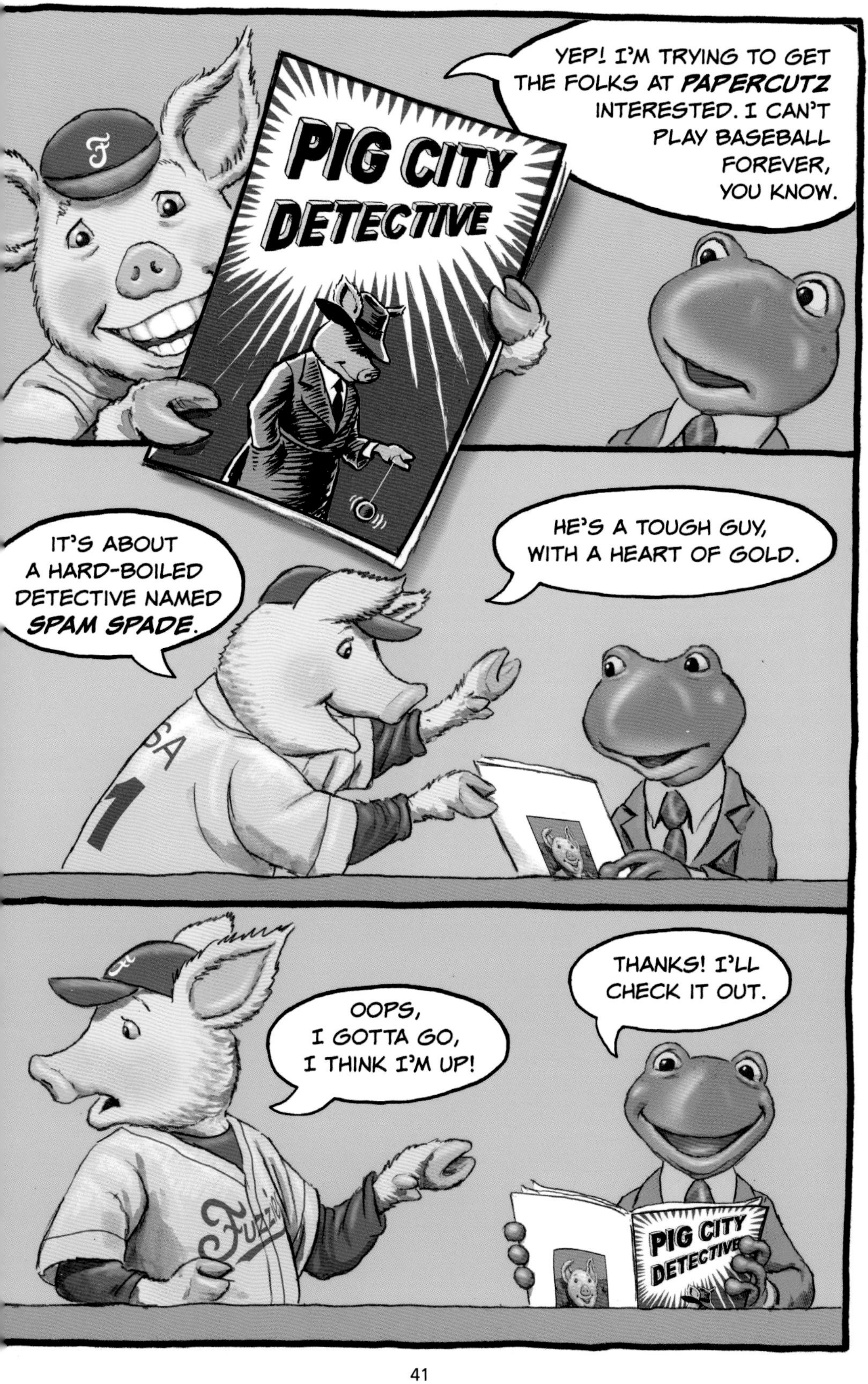
YEP! I'M TRYING TO GET THE FOLKS AT PAPERCUTZ INTERESTED. I CAN'T PLAY BASEBALL FOREVER, YOU KNOW.
PIG CITY DETECTIVE
IT'S ABOUT A HARD-BOILED DETECTIVE NAMED SPAM SPADE.
HE'S A TOUGH GUY, WITH A HEART OF GOLD.
OOPS, I GOTTA GO, I THINK I'M UP!
THANKS! I'LL CHECK IT OUT.
PIG CITY DETECTIVE

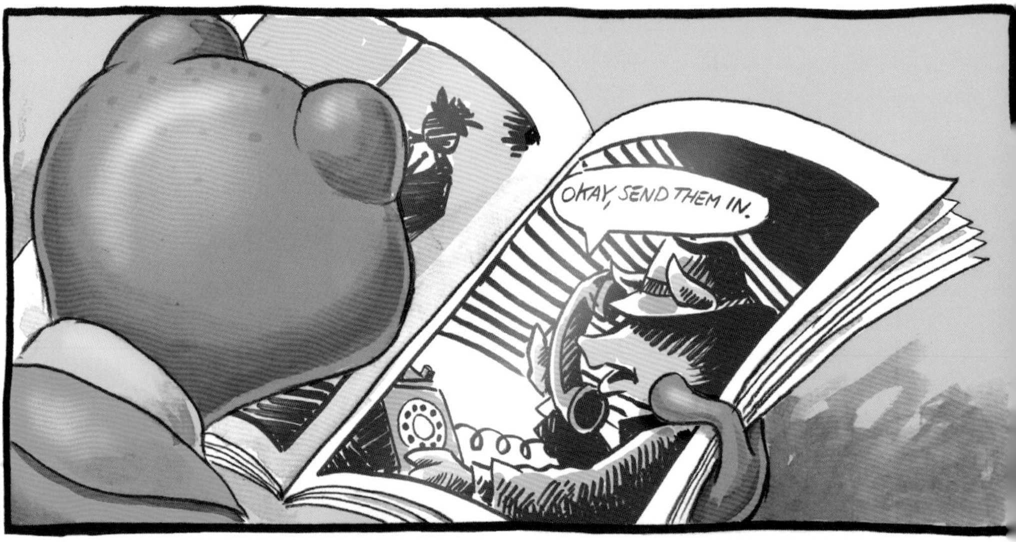
OKAY, SEND THEM IN.

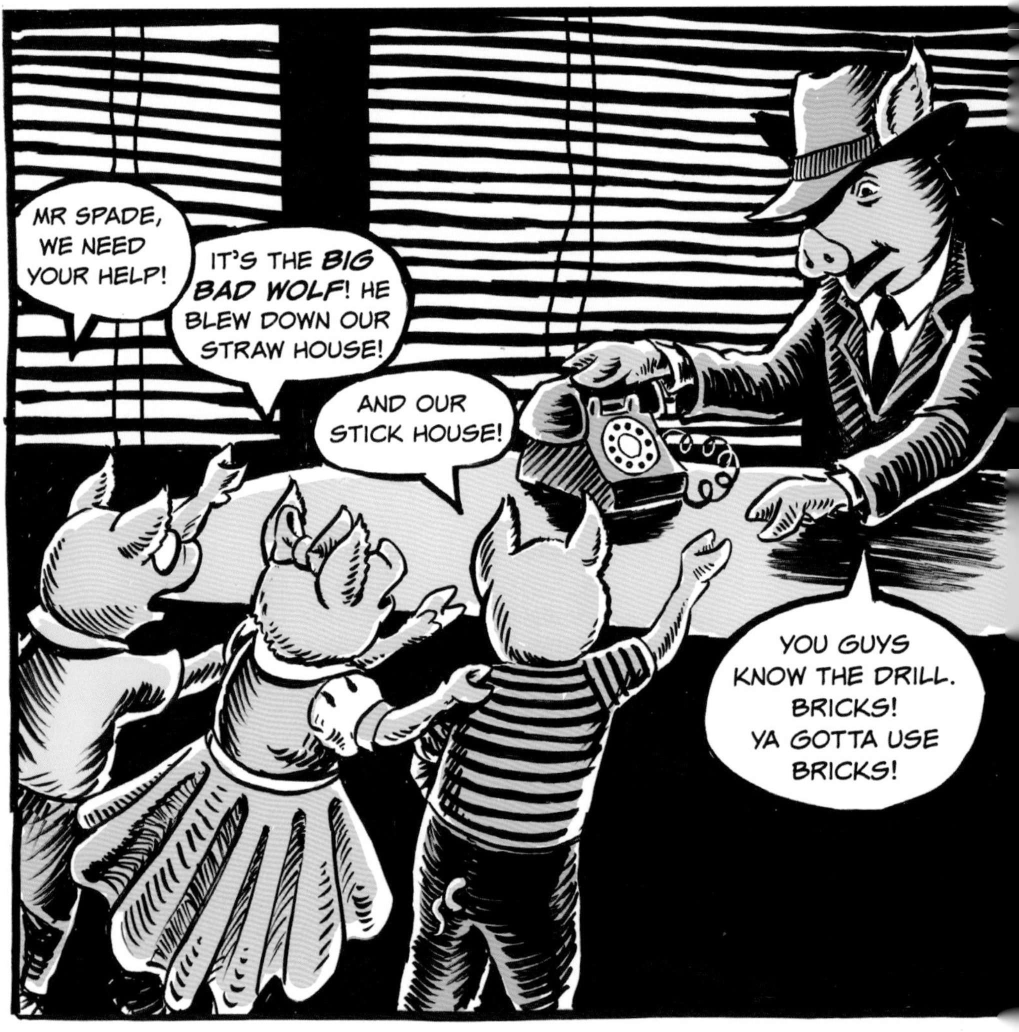
MR SPADE, WE NEED YOUR HELP!
IT'S THE **BIG BAD WOLF**! HE BLEW DOWN OUR STRAW HOUSE!
AND OUR STICK HOUSE!
YOU GUYS KNOW THE DRILL. BRICKS! YA GOTTA USE BRICKS!

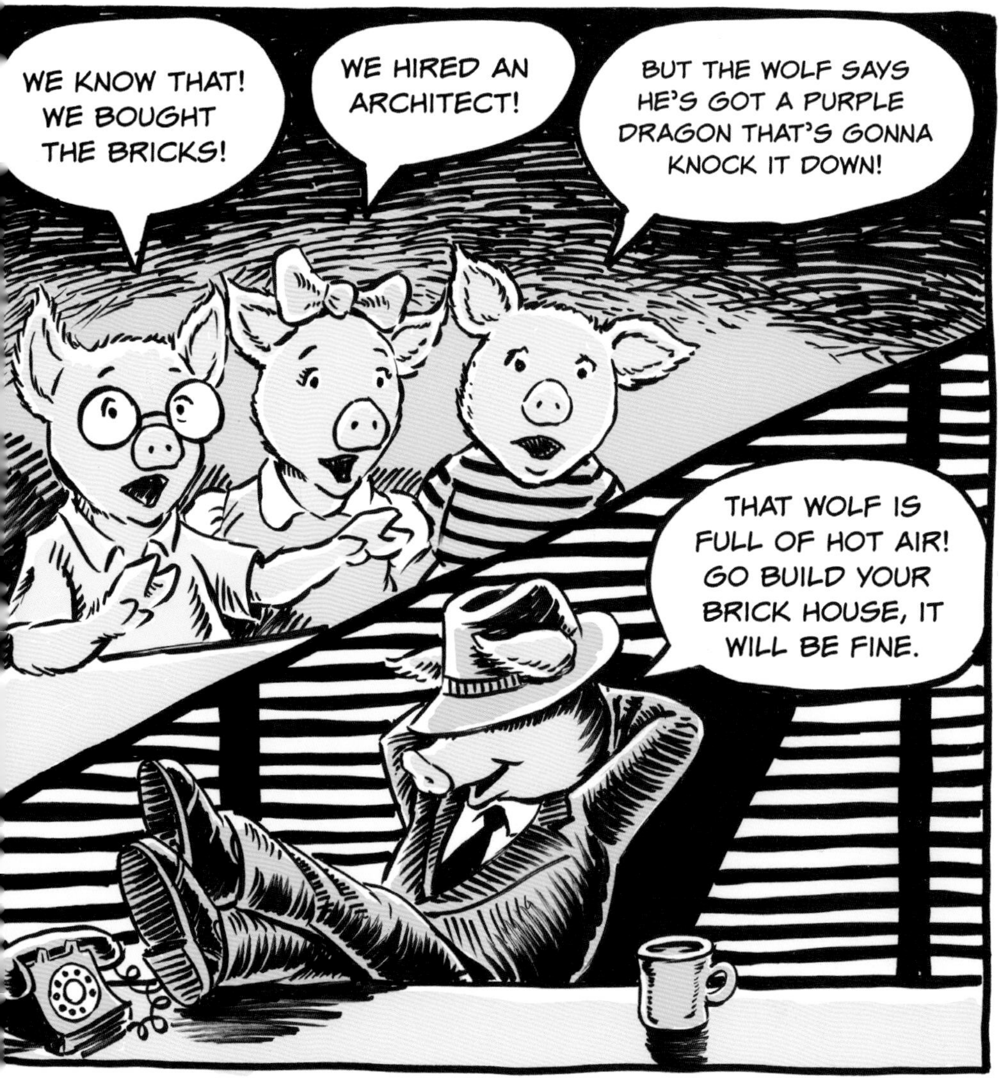
WE KNOW THAT! WE BOUGHT THE BRICKS!
WE HIRED AN ARCHITECT!
BUT THE WOLF SAYS HE'S GOT A PURPLE DRAGON THAT'S GONNA KNOCK IT DOWN!
THAT WOLF IS FULL OF HOT AIR! GO BUILD YOUR BRICK HOUSE, IT WILL BE FINE.

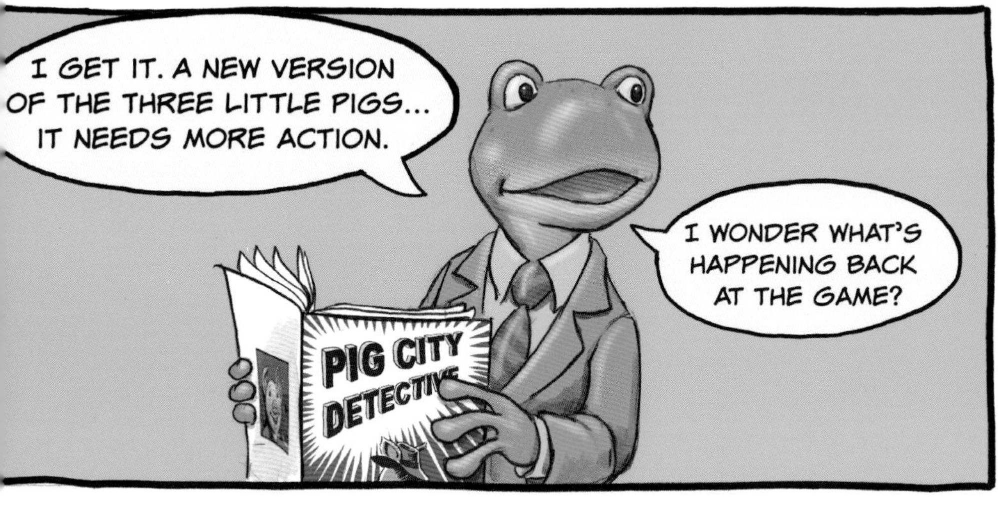
I GET IT. A NEW VERSION OF THE THREE LITTLE PIGS... IT NEEDS MORE ACTION.
I WONDER WHAT'S HAPPENING BACK AT THE GAME?
PIG CITY DETECTIVE

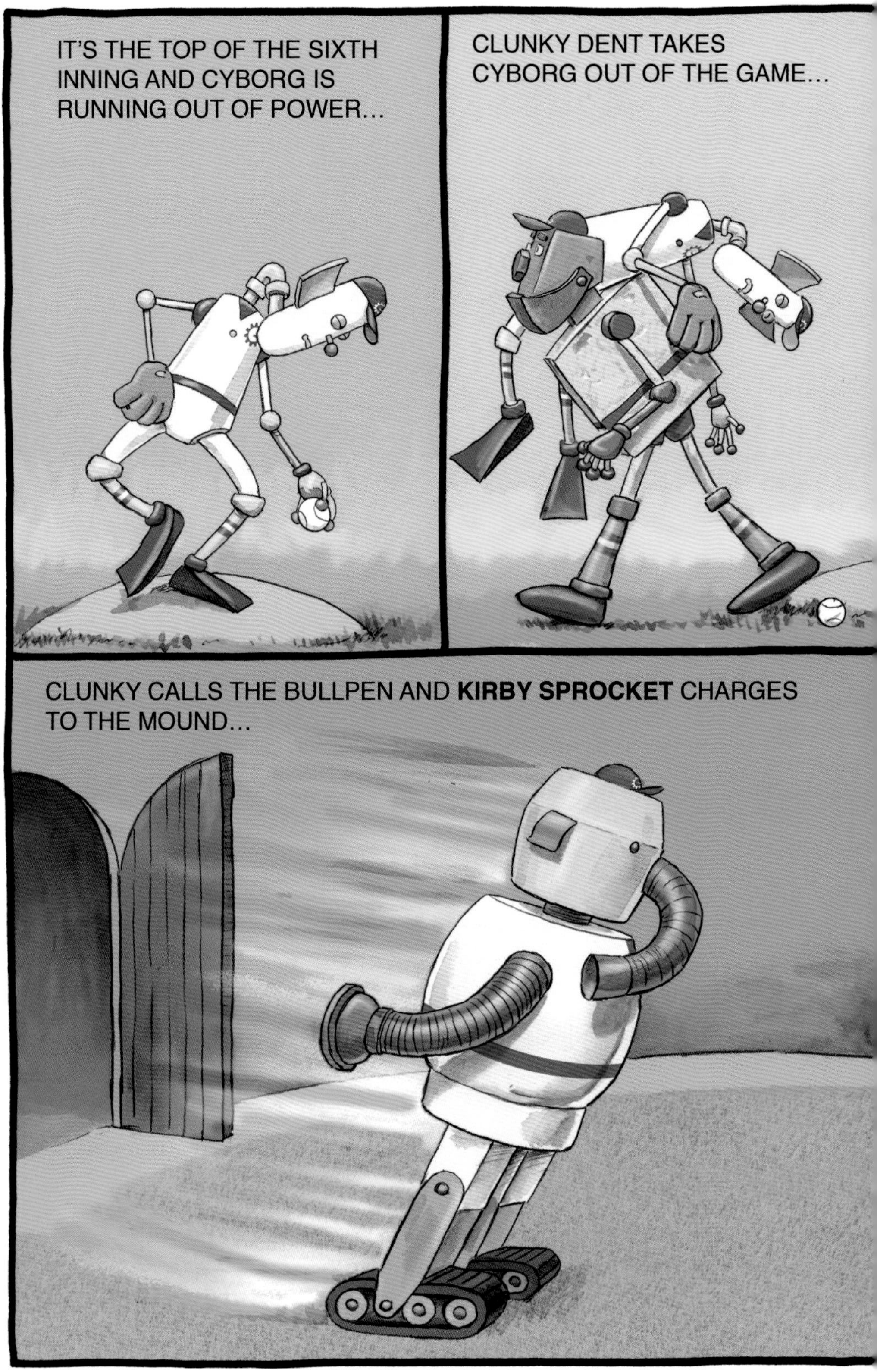
IT'S THE TOP OF THE SIXTH INNING AND CYBORG IS RUNNING OUT OF POWER...
CLUNKY DENT TAKES CYBORG OUT OF THE GAME...
CLUNKY CALLS THE BULLPEN AND **KIRBY SPROCKET** CHARGES TO THE MOUND...

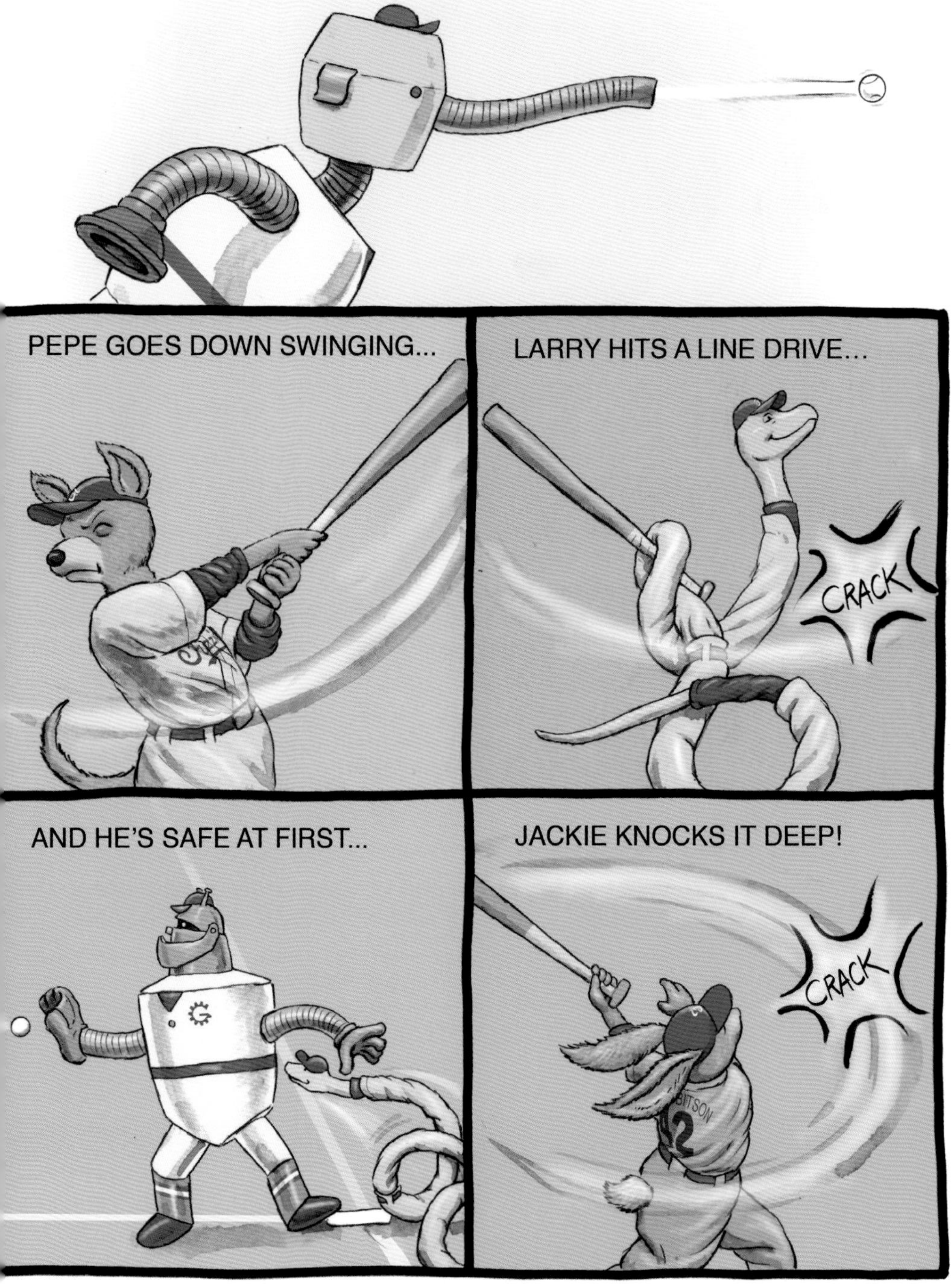
PEPE GOES DOWN SWINGING...
LARRY HITS A LINE DRIVE...
CRACK
AND HE'S SAFE AT FIRST...
JACKIE KNOCKS IT DEEP!
CRACK

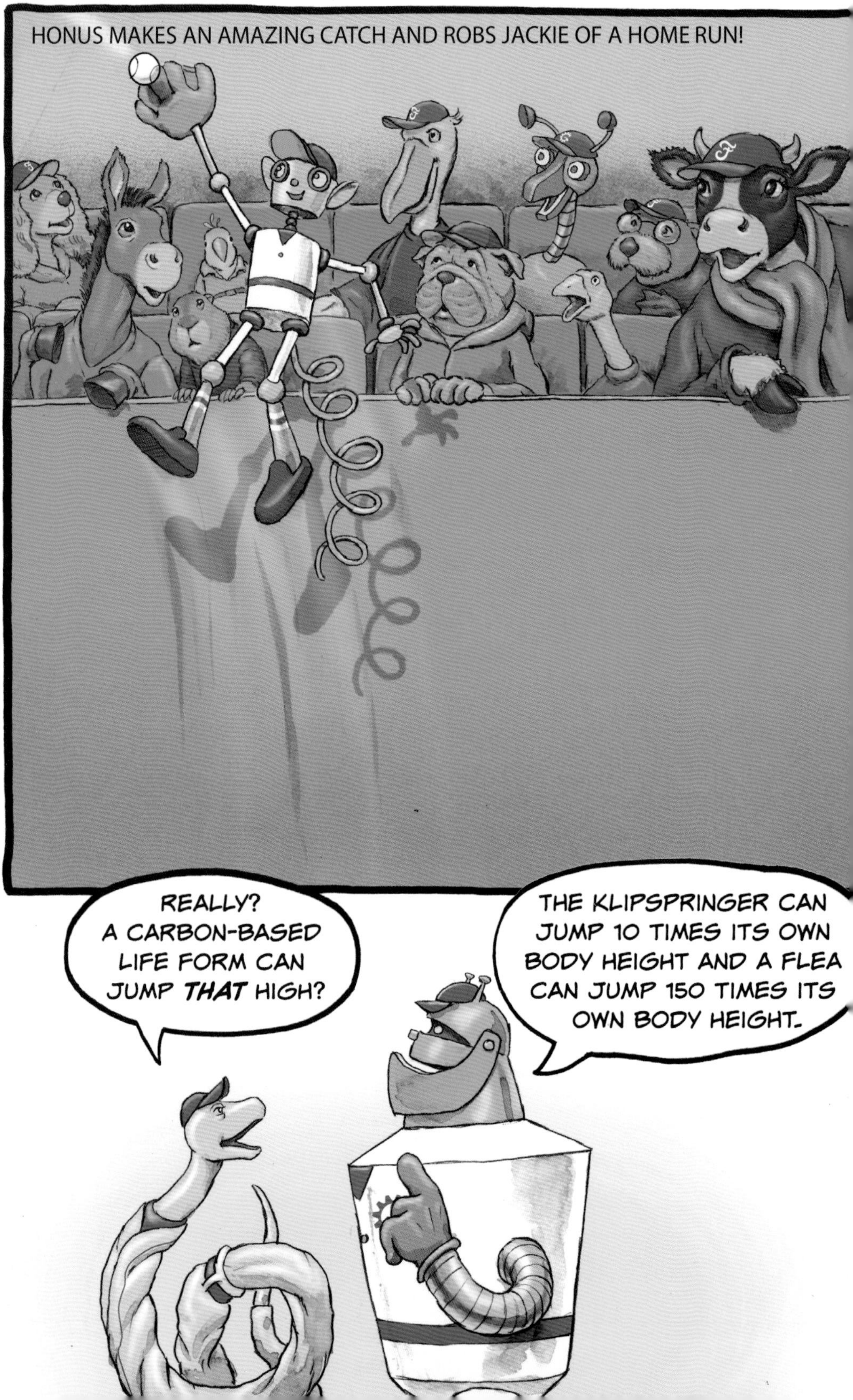
HONUS MAKES AN AMAZING CATCH AND ROBS JACKIE OF A HOME RUN!
REALLY? A CARBON-BASED LIFE FORM CAN JUMP *THAT* HIGH?
THE KLIPSPRINGER CAN JUMP 10 TIMES ITS OWN BODY HEIGHT AND A FLEA CAN JUMP 150 TIMES ITS OWN BODY HEIGHT.

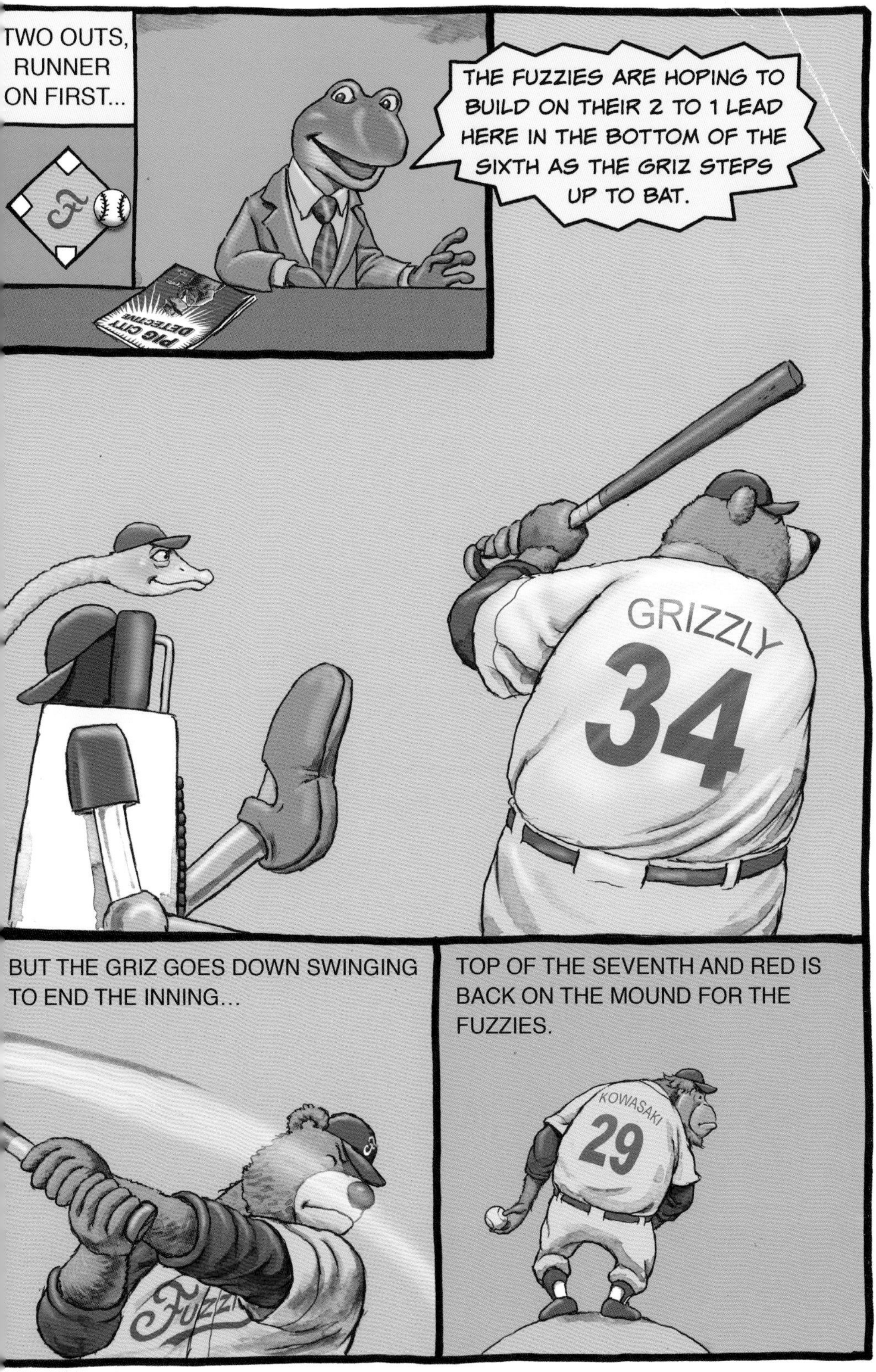
TWO OUTS, RUNNER ON FIRST...
THE FUZZIES ARE HOPING TO BUILD ON THEIR 2 TO 1 LEAD HERE IN THE BOTTOM OF THE SIXTH AS THE GRIZ STEPS UP TO BAT.
PIG CITY DETECTIVE
GRIZZLY
34
BUT THE GRIZ GOES DOWN SWINGING TO END THE INNING...
TOP OF THE SEVENTH AND RED IS BACK ON THE MOUND FOR THE FUZZIES.
KOWASAKI
29

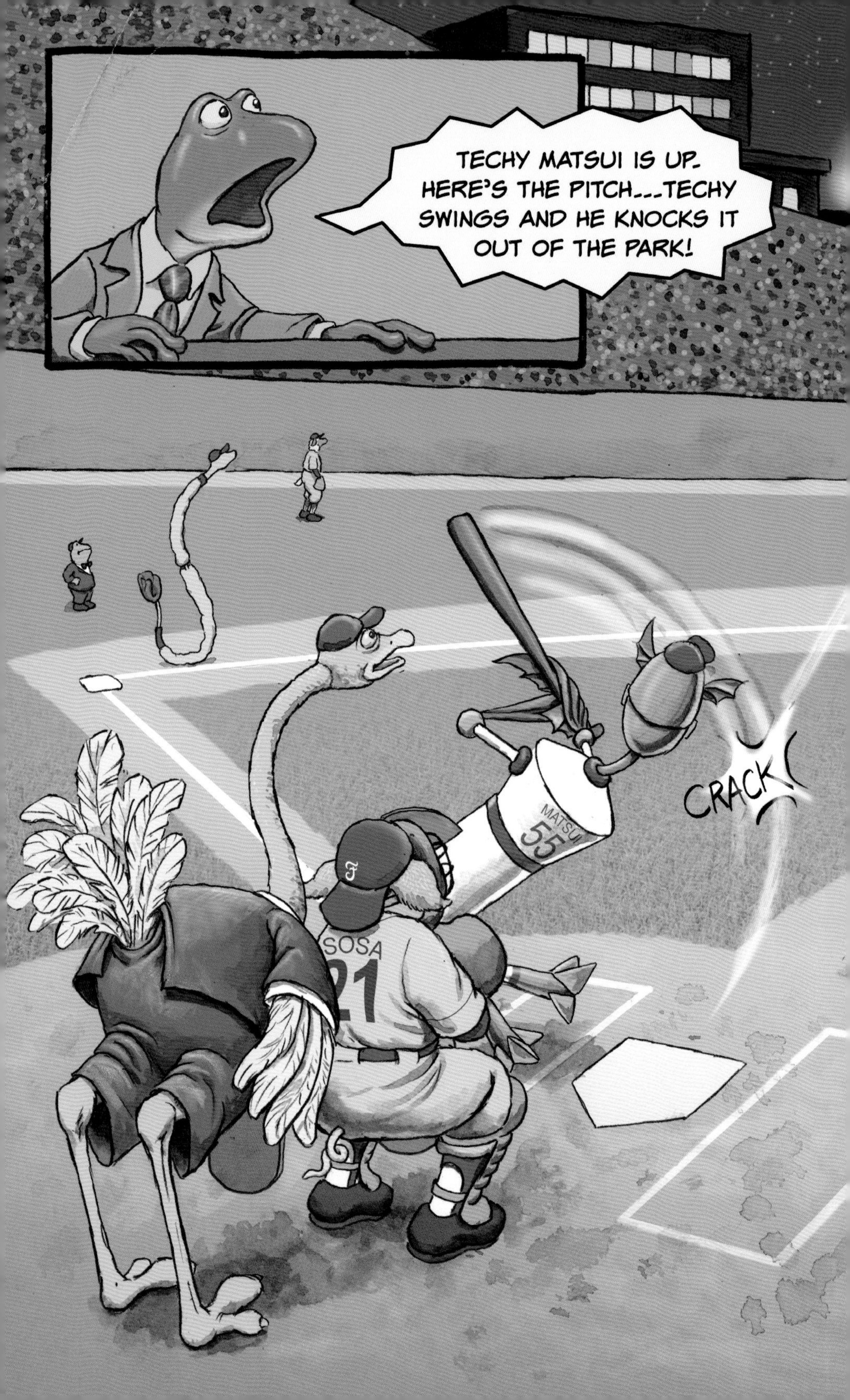
TECHY MATSUI IS UP. HERE'S THE PITCH...TECHY SWINGS AND HE KNOCKS IT OUT OF THE PARK!
MATSUI 55
SOSA 21
CRACK

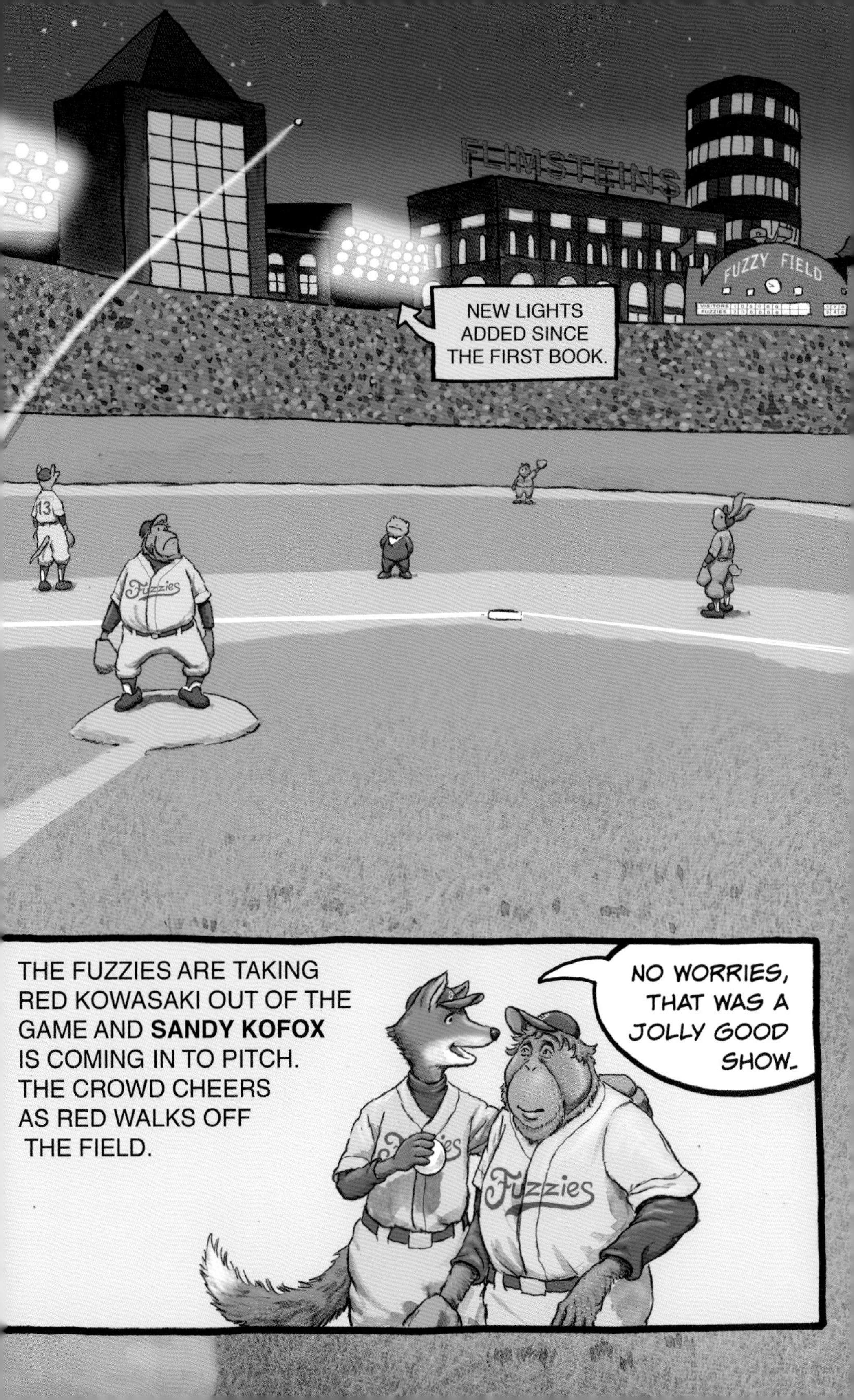
FLIMSTEINS
FUZZY FIELD
VISITORS
FUZZIES
NEW LIGHTS ADDED SINCE THE FIRST BOOK.
Fuzzies
THE FUZZIES ARE TAKING RED KOWASAKI OUT OF THE GAME AND **SANDY KOFOX** IS COMING IN TO PITCH. THE CROWD CHEERS AS RED WALKS OFF THE FIELD.
NO WORRIES, THAT WAS A JOLLY GOOD SHOW.
Fuzzies

SEVENTH INNING AND THE SCORE IS TIED AT 2 TO 2.
NO OUTS, AND THE CLANKEES ARE UP...

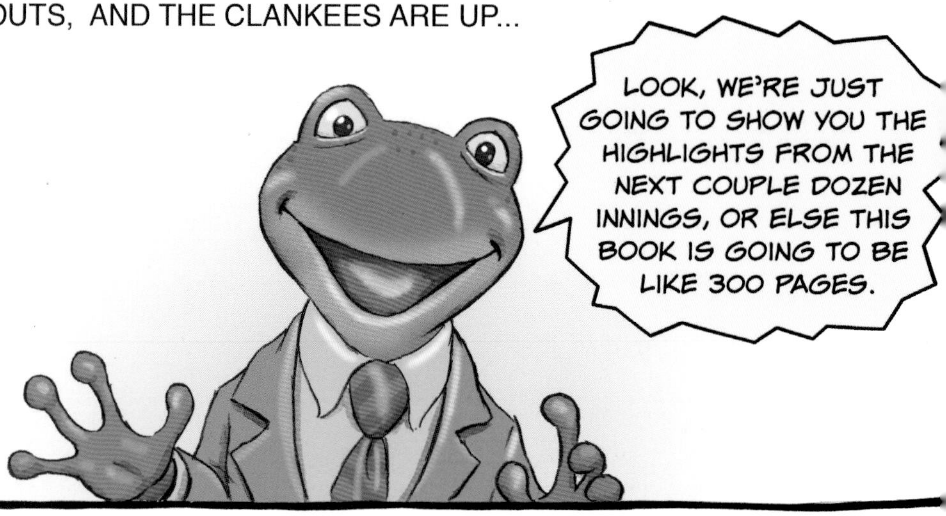
LOOK, WE'RE JUST GOING TO SHOW YOU THE HIGHLIGHTS FROM THE NEXT COUPLE DOZEN INNINGS, OR ELSE THIS BOOK IS GOING TO BE LIKE 300 PAGES.

EIGHTH INNING: HONUS WINGNUT RUNS OUT OF POWER AND IS REPLACED BY **LOU GEARIG**...

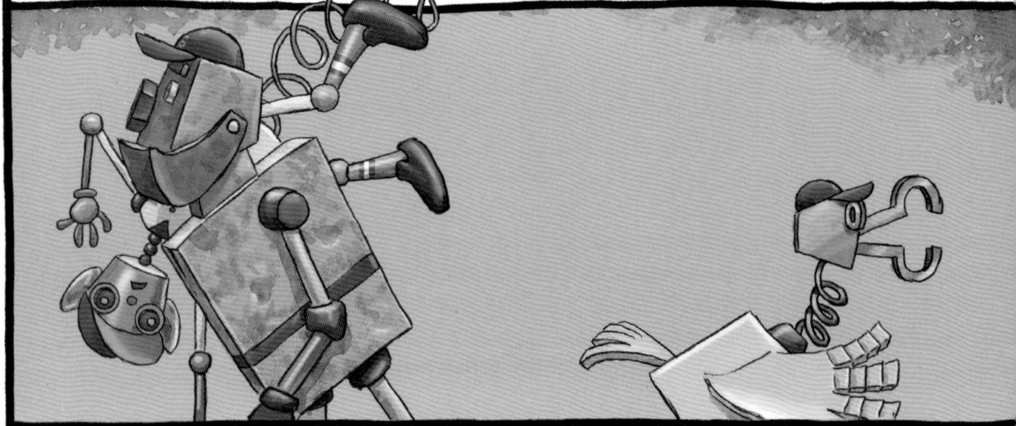

NINTH INNING: WALTER WOMBAT STRIKES OUT AND SENDS THE GAME INTO EXTRA INNINGS...

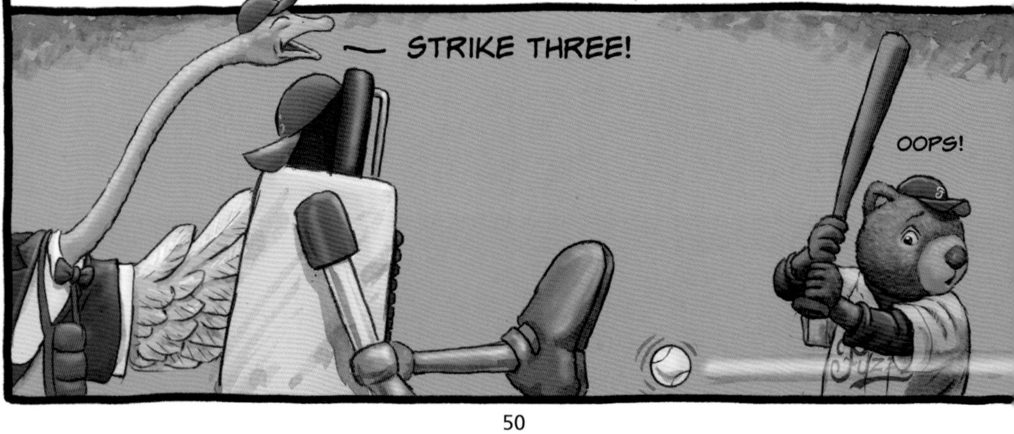
— STRIKE THREE!
OOPS!

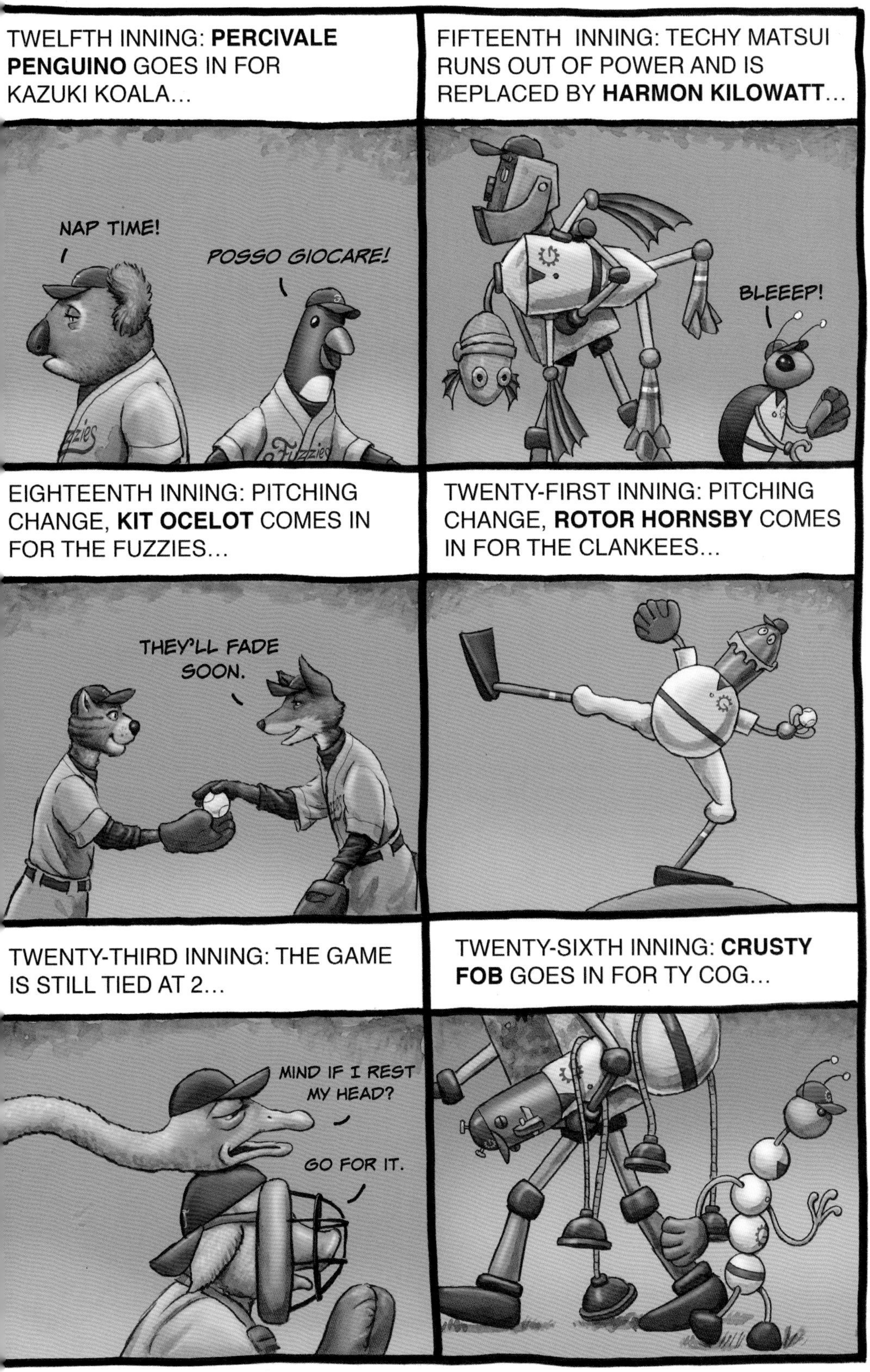
TWELFTH INNING: PERCIVALE PENGUINO GOES IN FOR KAZUKI KOALA…
NAP TIME!
POSSO GIOCARE!
FIFTEENTH INNING: TECHY MATSUI RUNS OUT OF POWER AND IS REPLACED BY HARMON KILOWATT…
BLEEEP!
EIGHTEENTH INNING: PITCHING CHANGE, KIT OCELOT COMES IN FOR THE FUZZIES…
THEY'LL FADE SOON.
TWENTY-FIRST INNING: PITCHING CHANGE, ROTOR HORNSBY COMES IN FOR THE CLANKEES…
TWENTY-THIRD INNING: THE GAME IS STILL TIED AT 2…
MIND IF I REST MY HEAD?
GO FOR IT.
TWENTY-SIXTH INNING: CRUSTY FOB GOES IN FOR TY COG…

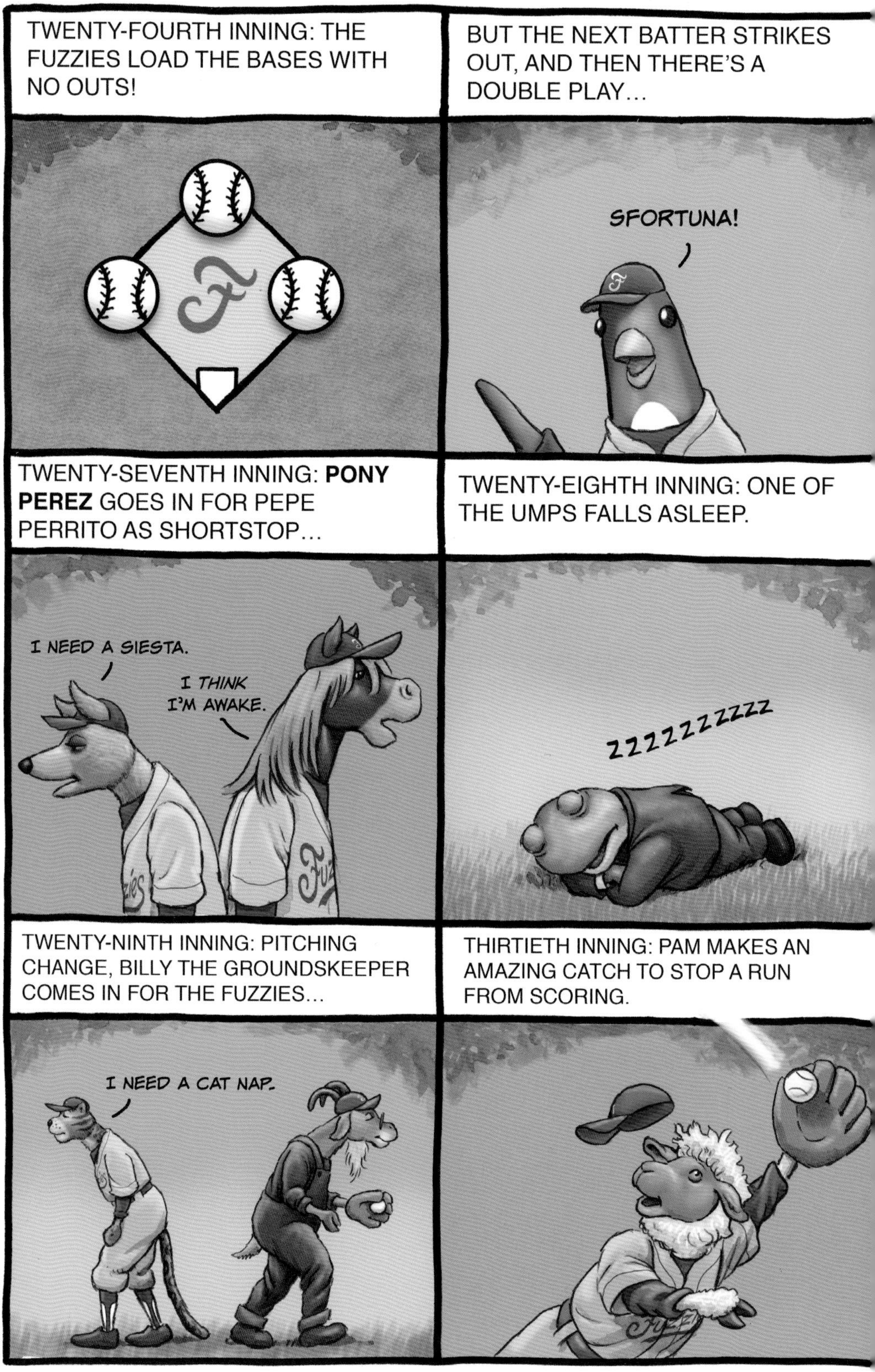
TWENTY-FOURTH INNING: THE FUZZIES LOAD THE BASES WITH NO OUTS!
BUT THE NEXT BATTER STRIKES OUT, AND THEN THERE'S A DOUBLE PLAY…
SFORTUNA!
TWENTY-SEVENTH INNING: **PONY PEREZ** GOES IN FOR PEPE PERRITO AS SHORTSTOP…
I NEED A SIESTA.
I *THINK* I'M AWAKE.
TWENTY-EIGHTH INNING: ONE OF THE UMPS FALLS ASLEEP.
ZZZZZZZZZZ
TWENTY-NINTH INNING: PITCHING CHANGE, BILLY THE GROUNDSKEEPER COMES IN FOR THE FUZZIES…
I NEED A CAT NAP.
THIRTIETH INNING: PAM MAKES AN AMAZING CATCH TO STOP A RUN FROM SCORING.

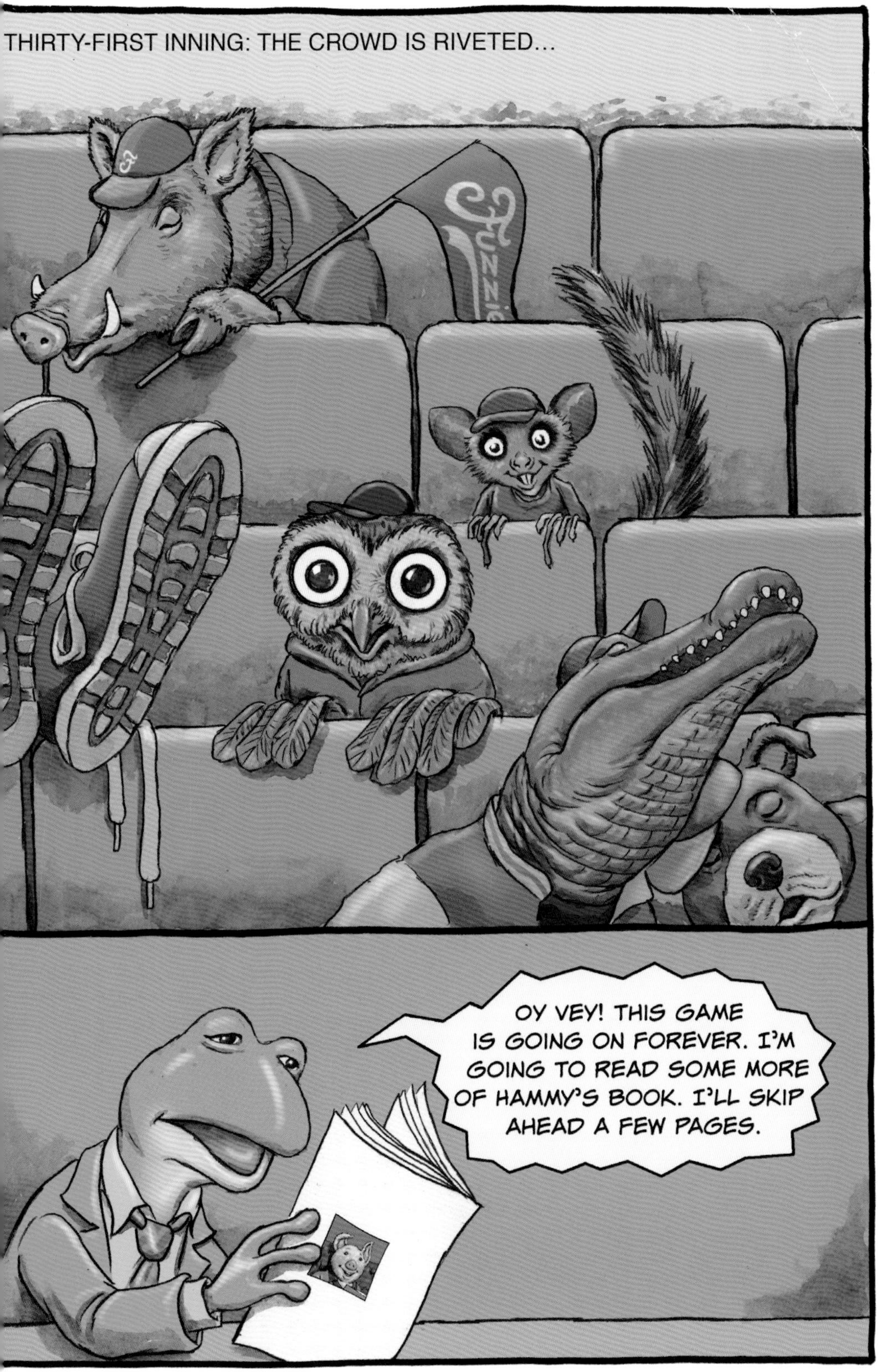
THIRTY-FIRST INNING: THE CROWD IS RIVETED...
OY VEY! THIS GAME IS GOING ON FOREVER. I'M GOING TO READ SOME MORE OF HAMMY'S BOOK. I'LL SKIP AHEAD A FEW PAGES.

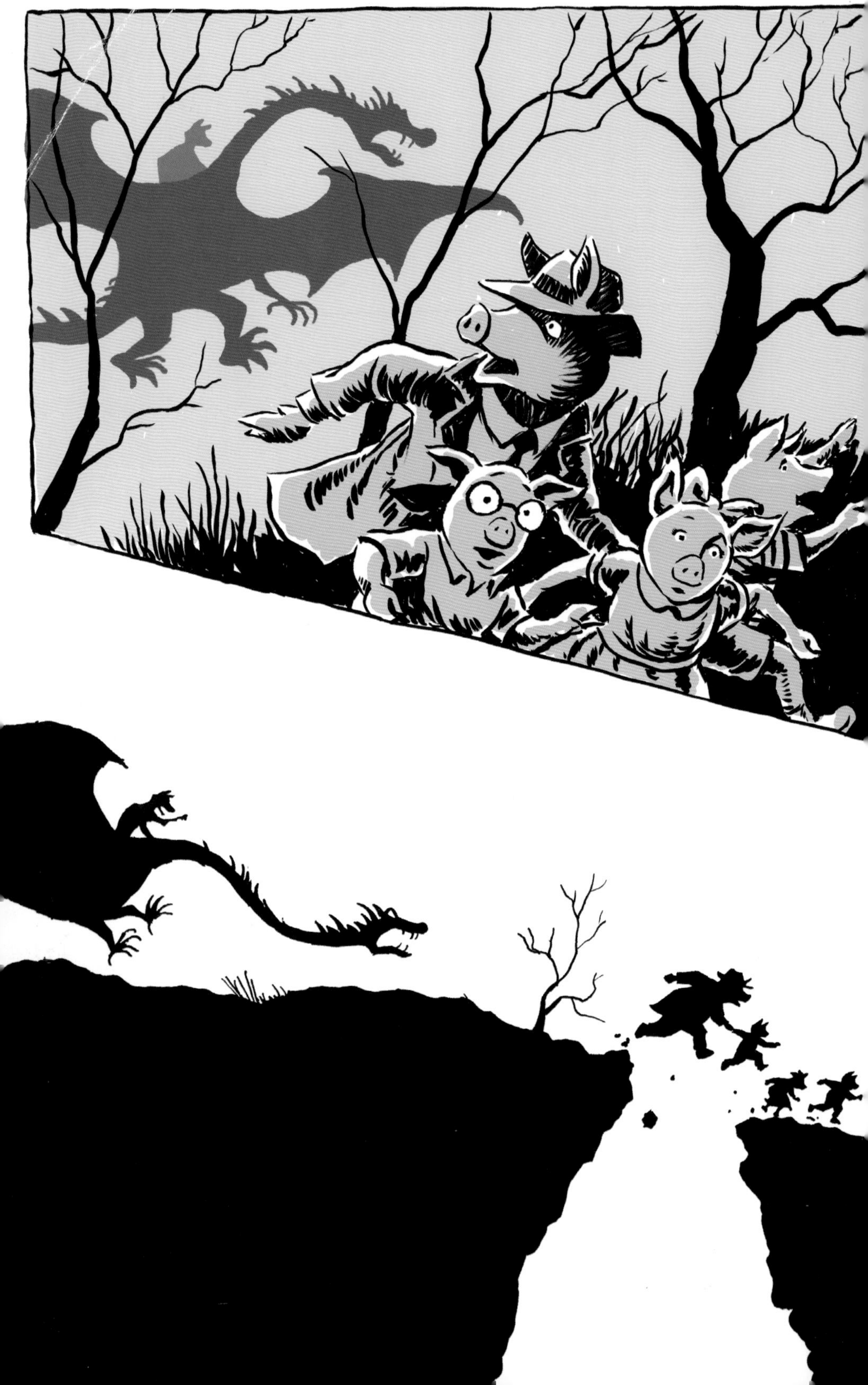

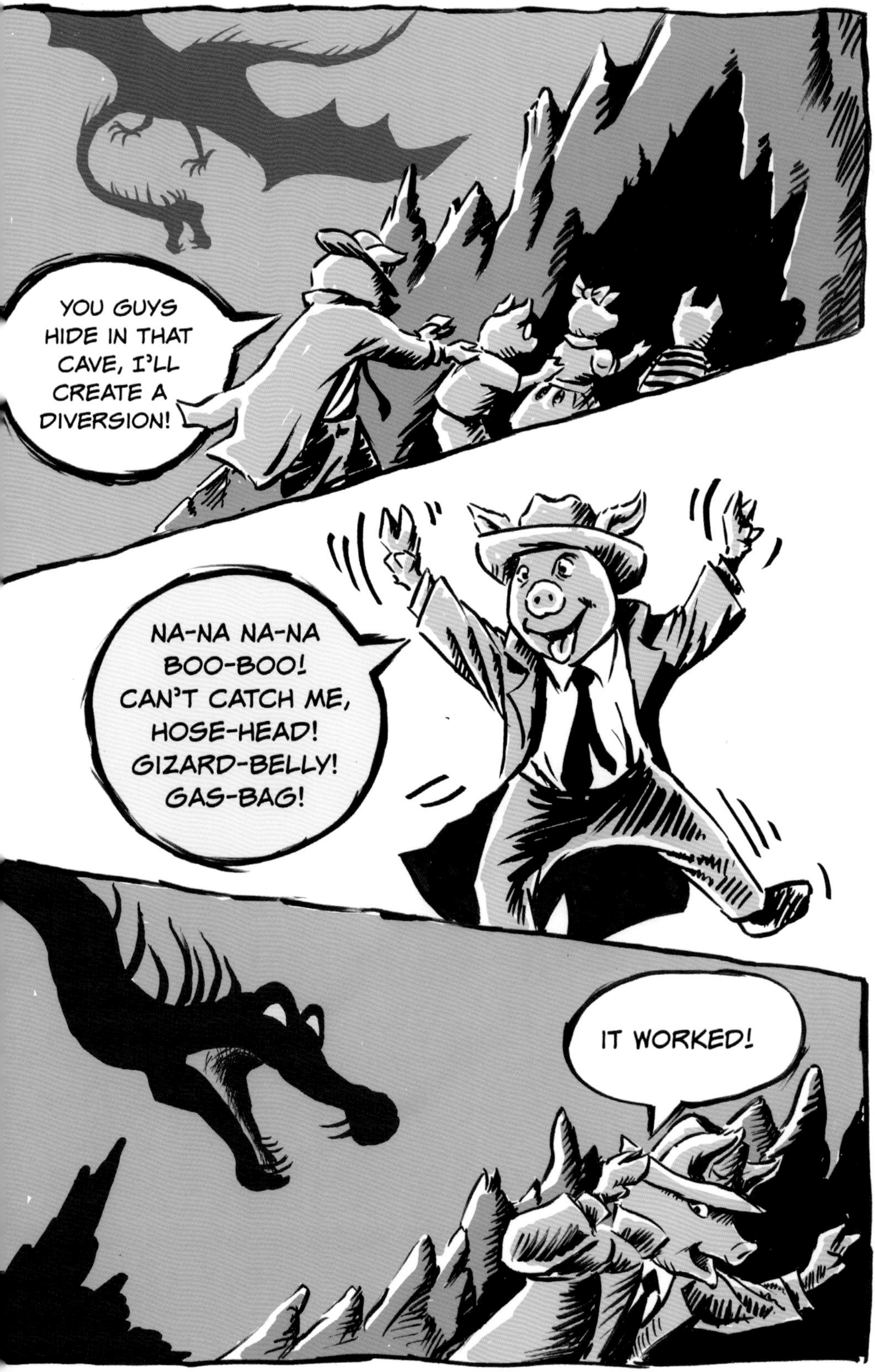
YOU GUYS HIDE IN THAT CAVE, I'LL CREATE A DIVERSION!
NA-NA NA-NA BOO-BOO! CAN'T CATCH ME, HOSE-HEAD! GIZARD-BELLY! GAS-BAG!
IT WORKED!

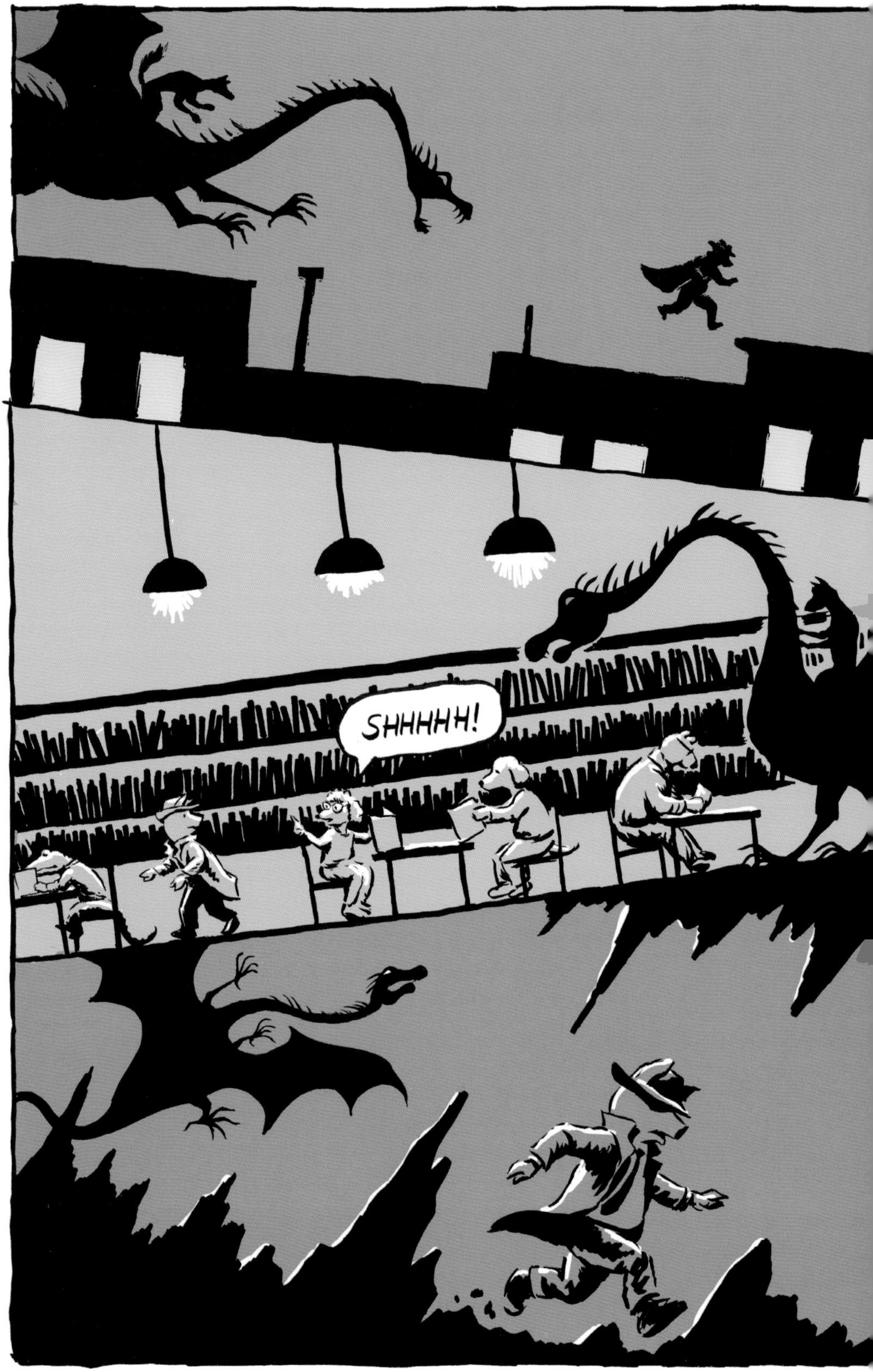
SHHHHH!

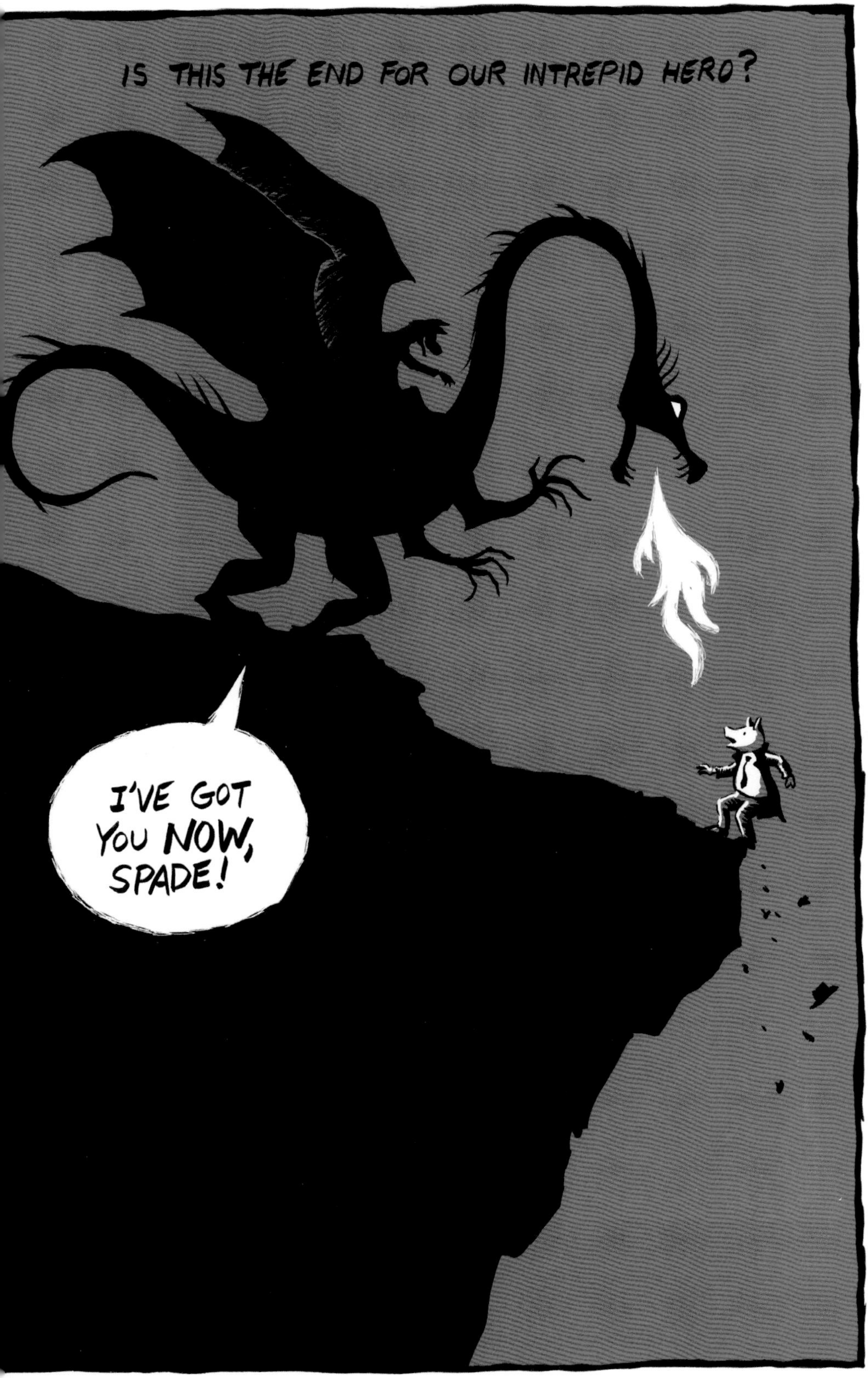
IS THIS THE END FOR OUR INTREPID HERO?
I'VE GOT YOU NOW, SPADE!

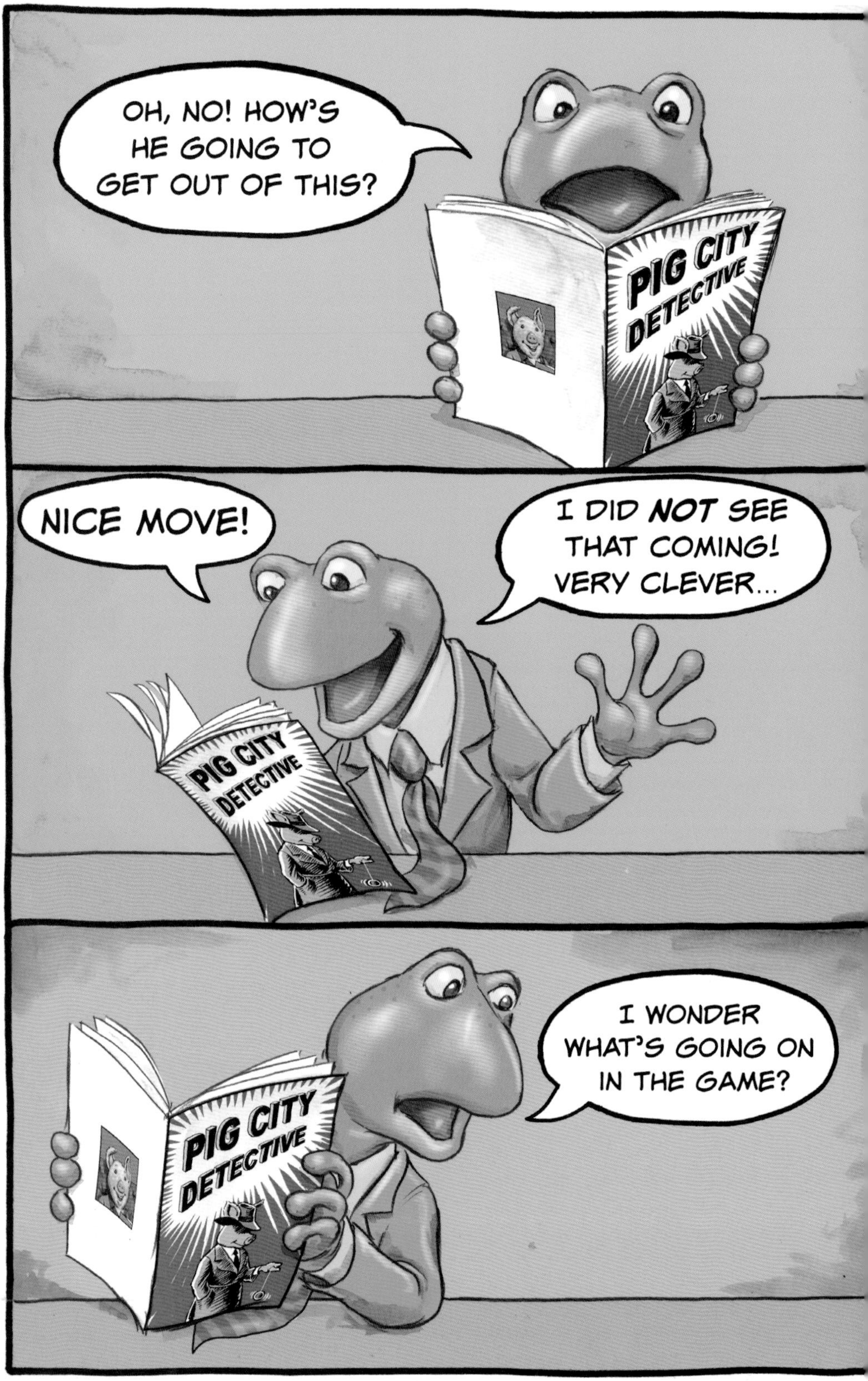
OH, NO! HOW'S HE GOING TO GET OUT OF THIS?
PIG CITY DETECTIVE
NICE MOVE!
I DID **NOT** SEE THAT COMING! VERY CLEVER...
PIG CITY DETECTIVE
PIG CITY DETECTIVE
I WONDER WHAT'S GOING ON IN THE GAME?

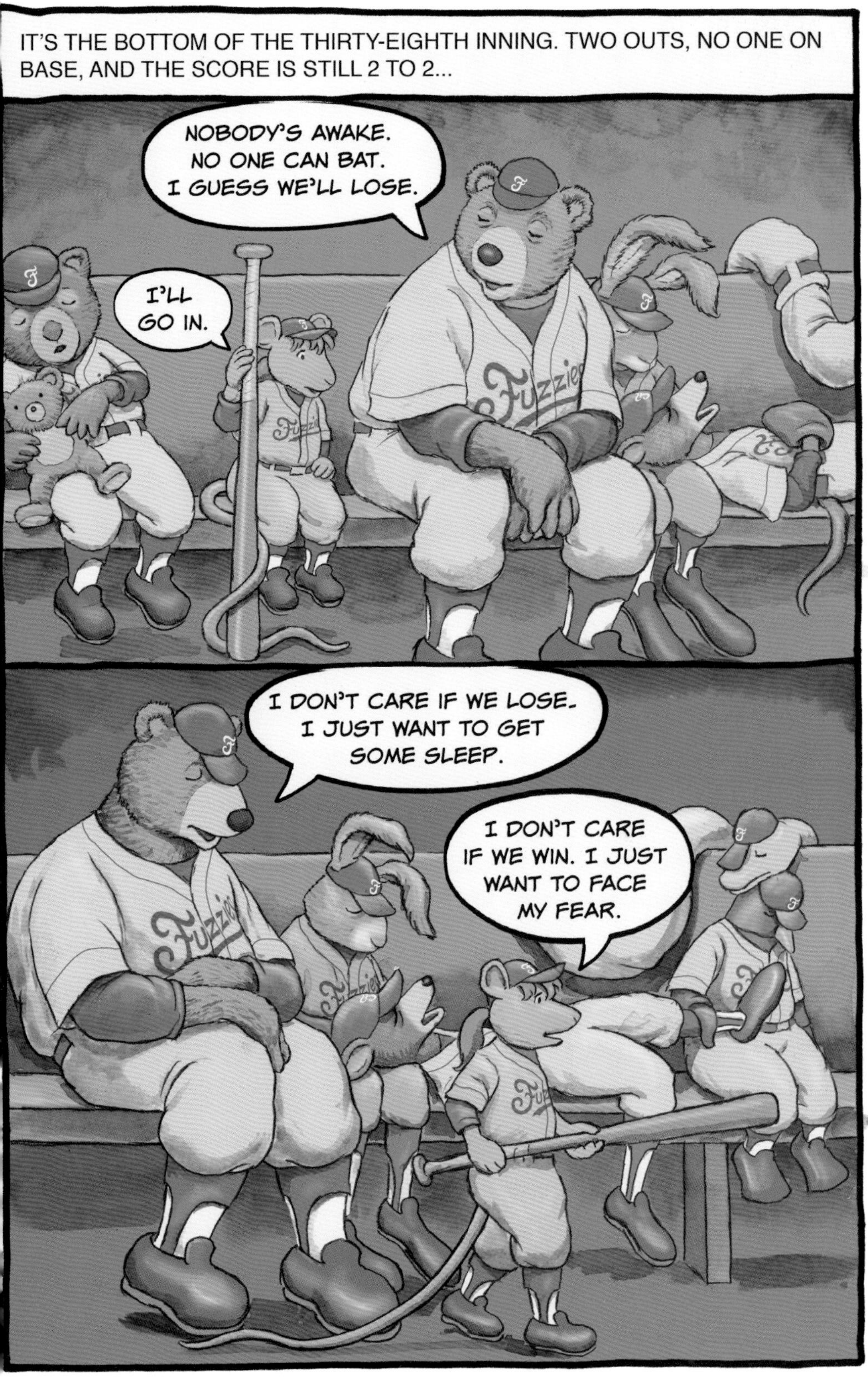
IT'S THE BOTTOM OF THE THIRTY-EIGHTH INNING. TWO OUTS, NO ONE ON BASE, AND THE SCORE IS STILL 2 TO 2...
NOBODY'S AWAKE. NO ONE CAN BAT. I GUESS WE'LL LOSE.
I'LL GO IN.
I DON'T CARE IF WE LOSE. I JUST WANT TO GET SOME SLEEP.
I DON'T CARE IF WE WIN. I JUST WANT TO FACE MY FEAR.

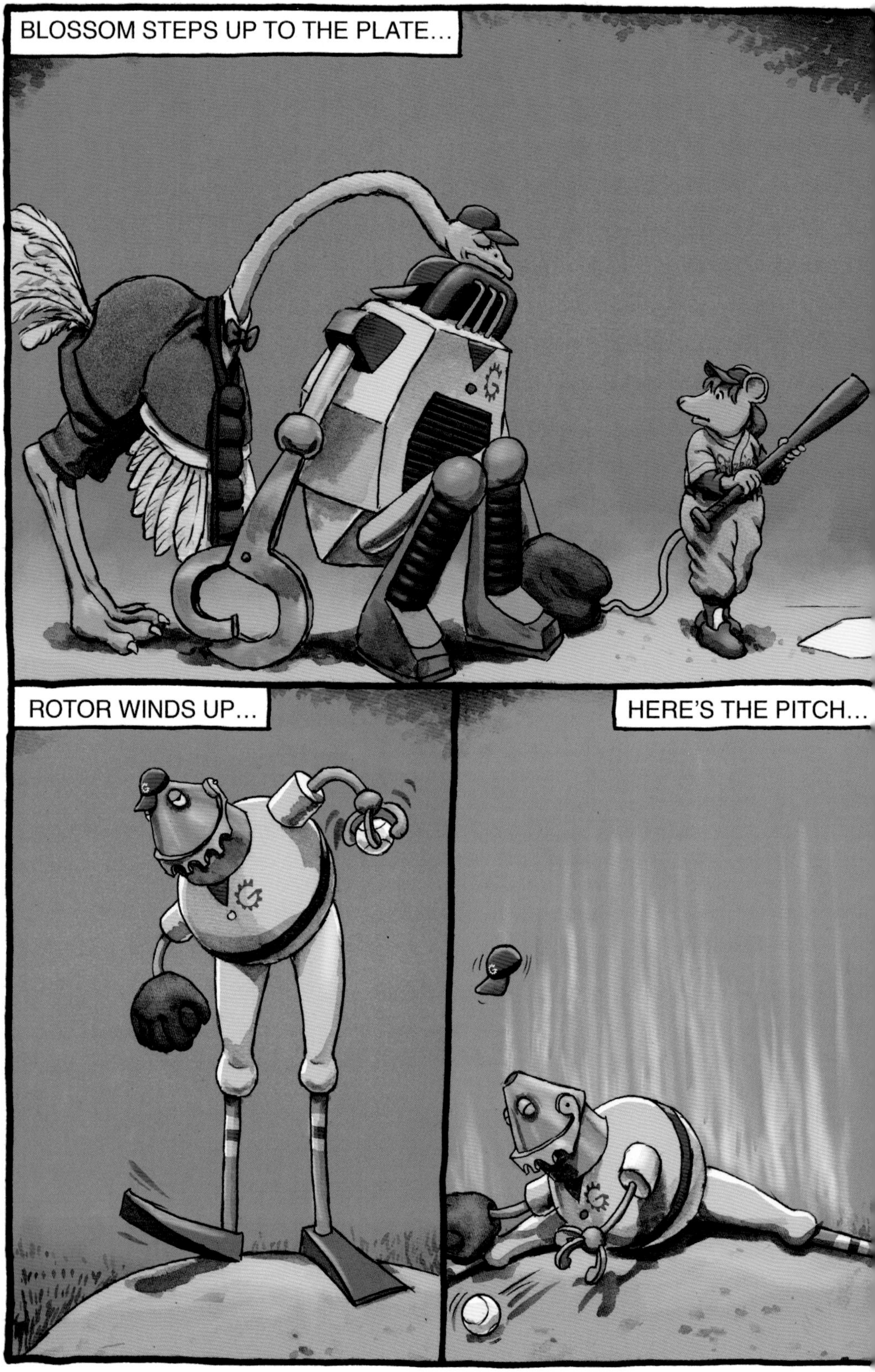
BLOSSOM STEPS UP TO THE PLATE...
ROTOR WINDS UP...
HERE'S THE PITCH...

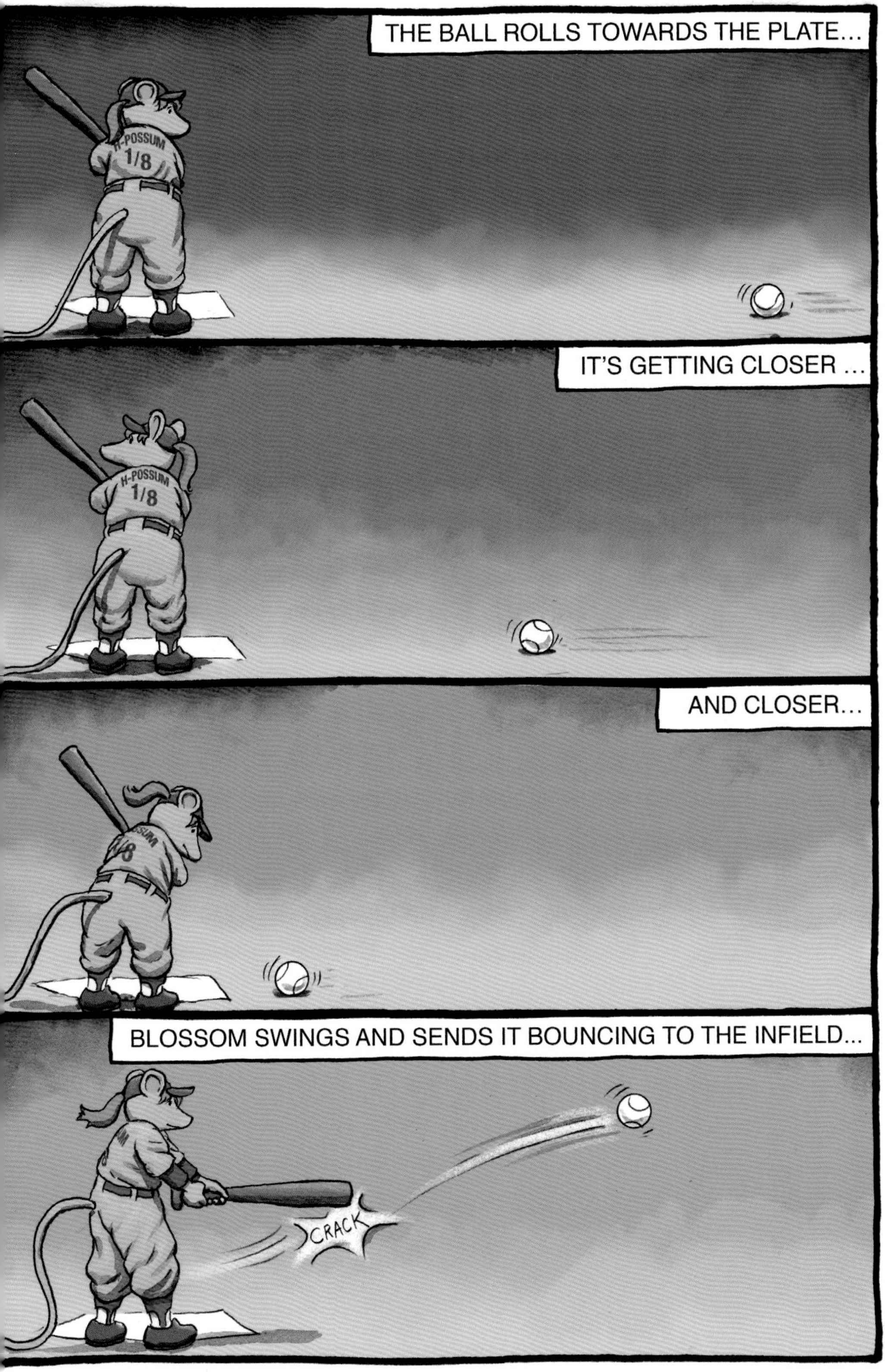
THE BALL ROLLS TOWARDS THE PLATE…
H-POSSUM
1/8
IT'S GETTING CLOSER …
H-POSSUM
1/8
AND CLOSER…
BLOSSOM SWINGS AND SENDS IT BOUNCING TO THE INFIELD…
CRACK

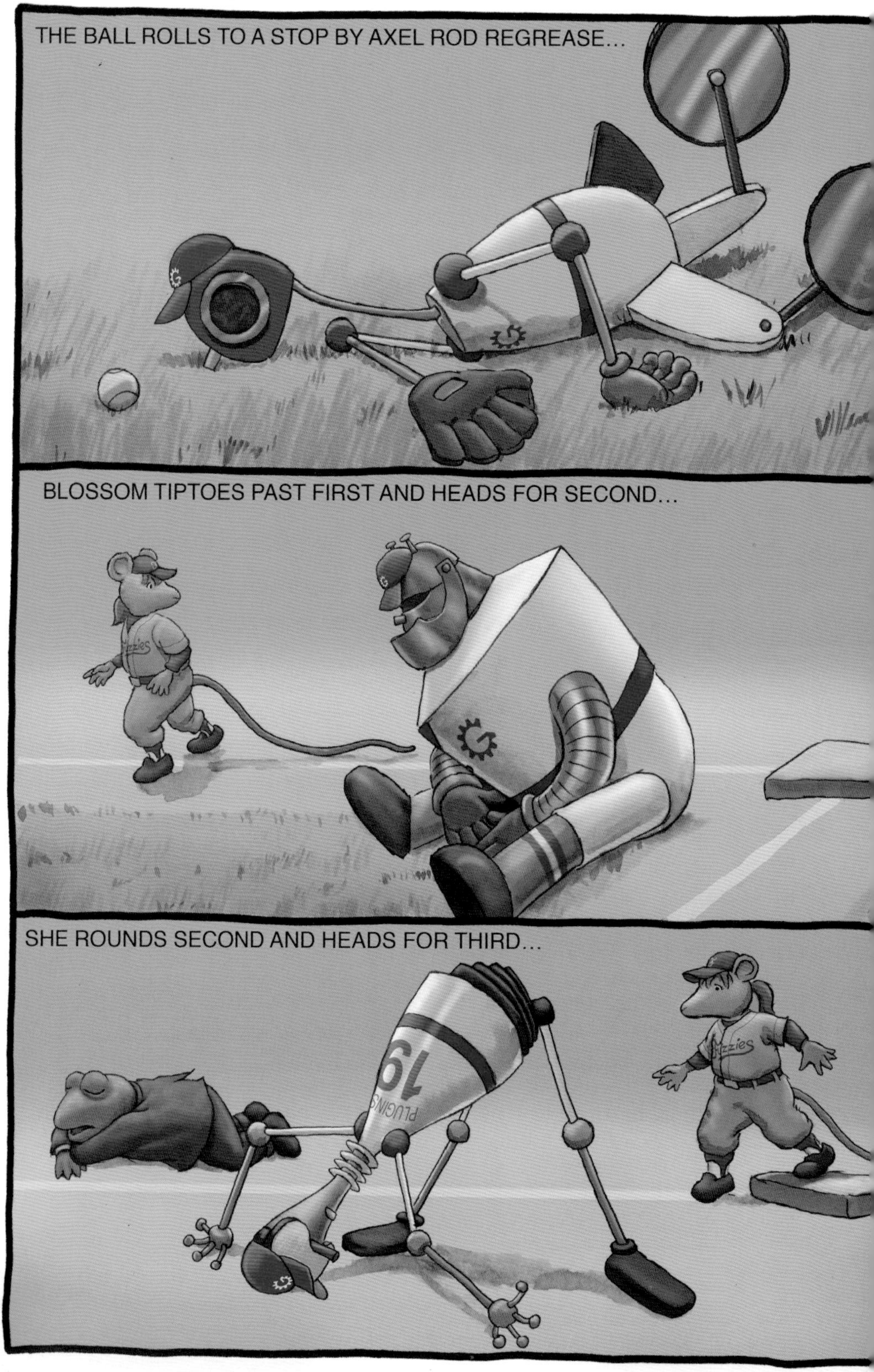
THE BALL ROLLS TO A STOP BY AXEL ROD REGREASE...
BLOSSOM TIPTOES PAST FIRST AND HEADS FOR SECOND...
SHE ROUNDS SECOND AND HEADS FOR THIRD...

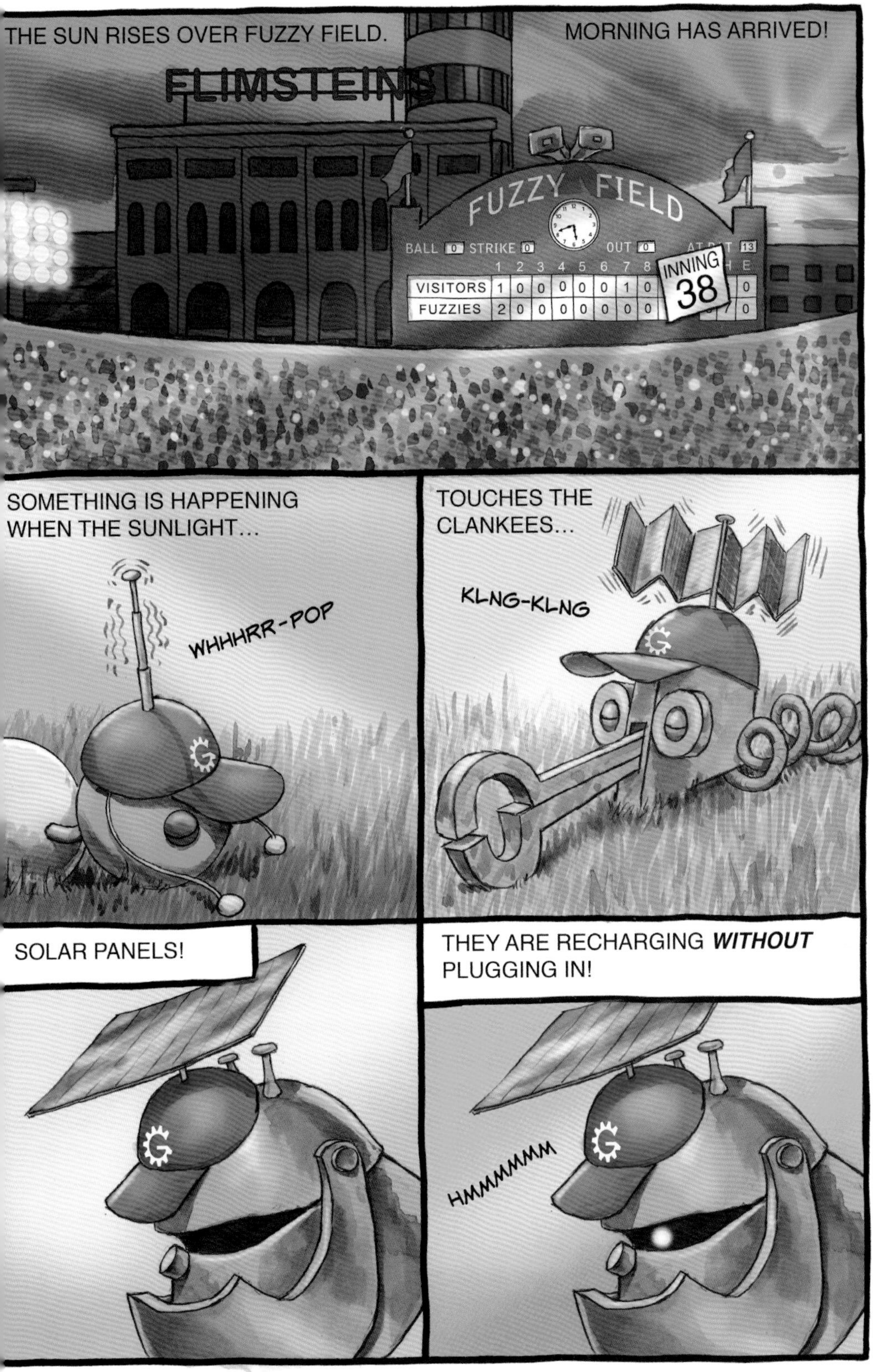
THE SUN RISES OVER FUZZY FIELD.
MORNING HAS ARRIVED!
FLIMSTEINS
FUZZY FIELD
BALL 0 STRIKE 0
OUT 0
INNING 38
VISITORS
FUZZIES
SOMETHING IS HAPPENING WHEN THE SUNLIGHT...
WHHHRR-POP
TOUCHES THE CLANKEES...
KLNG-KLNG
SOLAR PANELS!
THEY ARE RECHARGING *WITHOUT* PLUGGING IN!
HMMMMMM

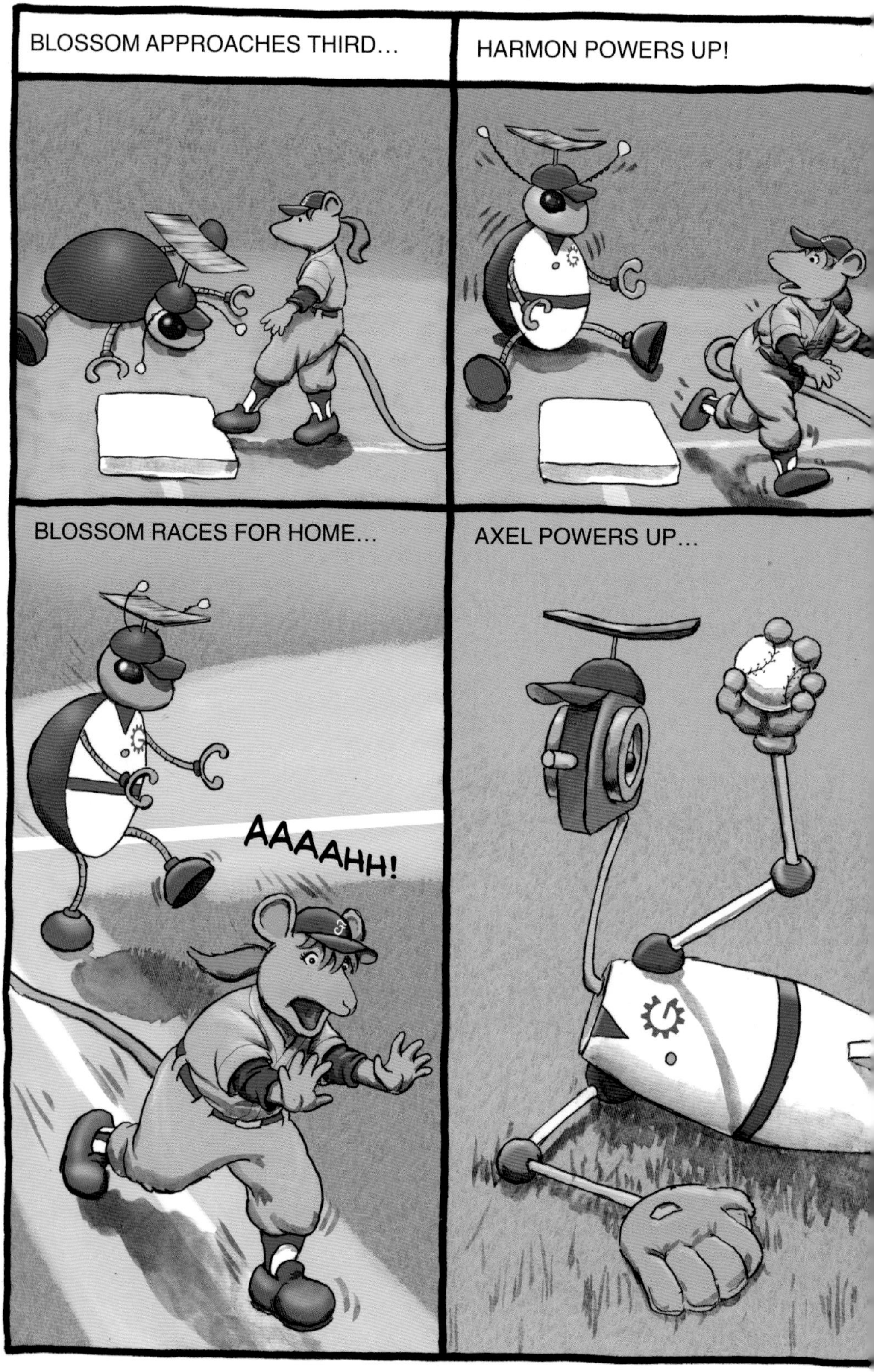
BLOSSOM APPROACHES THIRD...
HARMON POWERS UP!
BLOSSOM RACES FOR HOME...
AAAAHH!
AXEL POWERS UP...

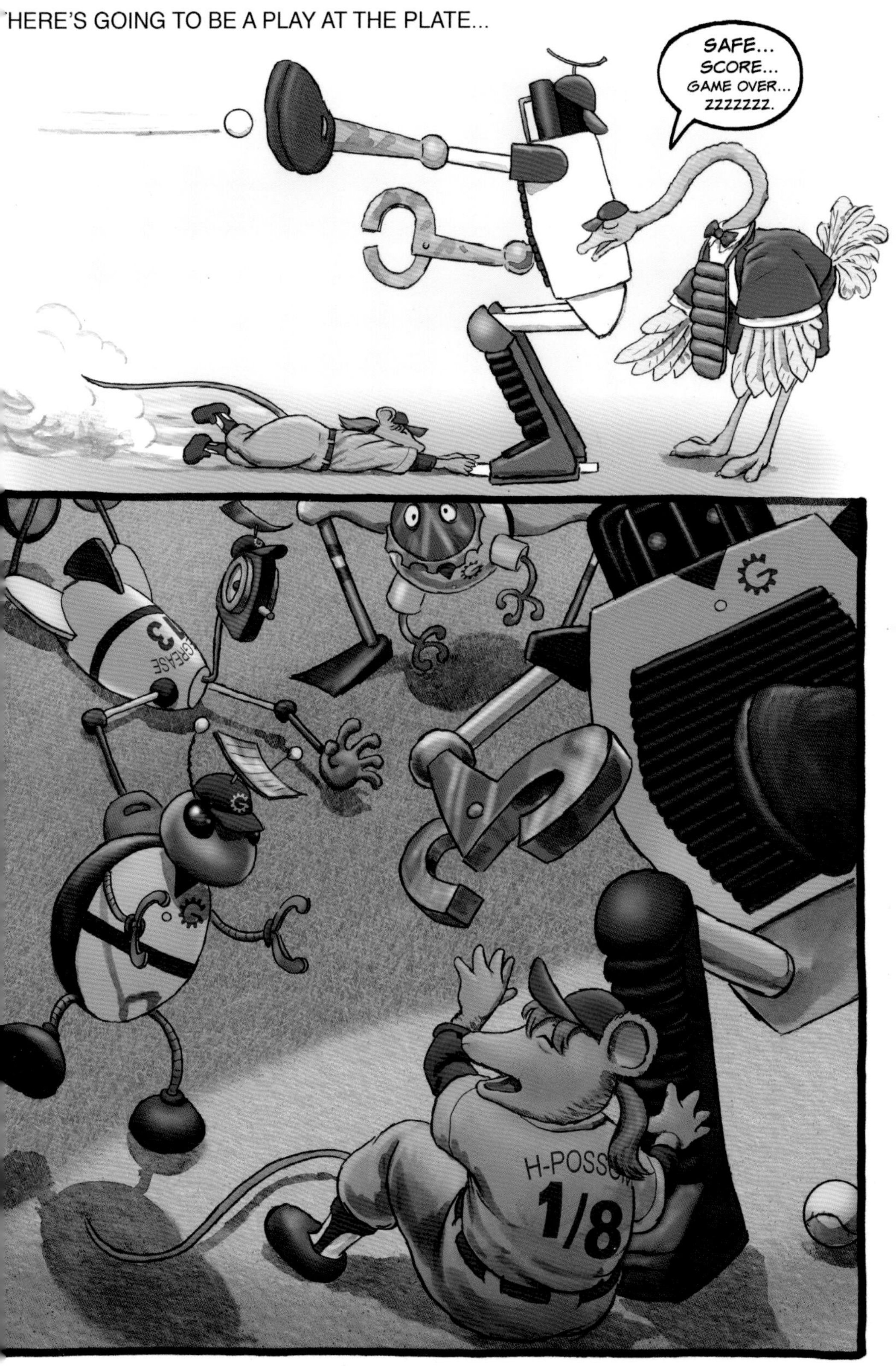
HERE'S GOING TO BE A PLAY AT THE PLATE...
SAFE... SCORE... GAME OVER... ZZZZZZZ.
GREASE
1/8

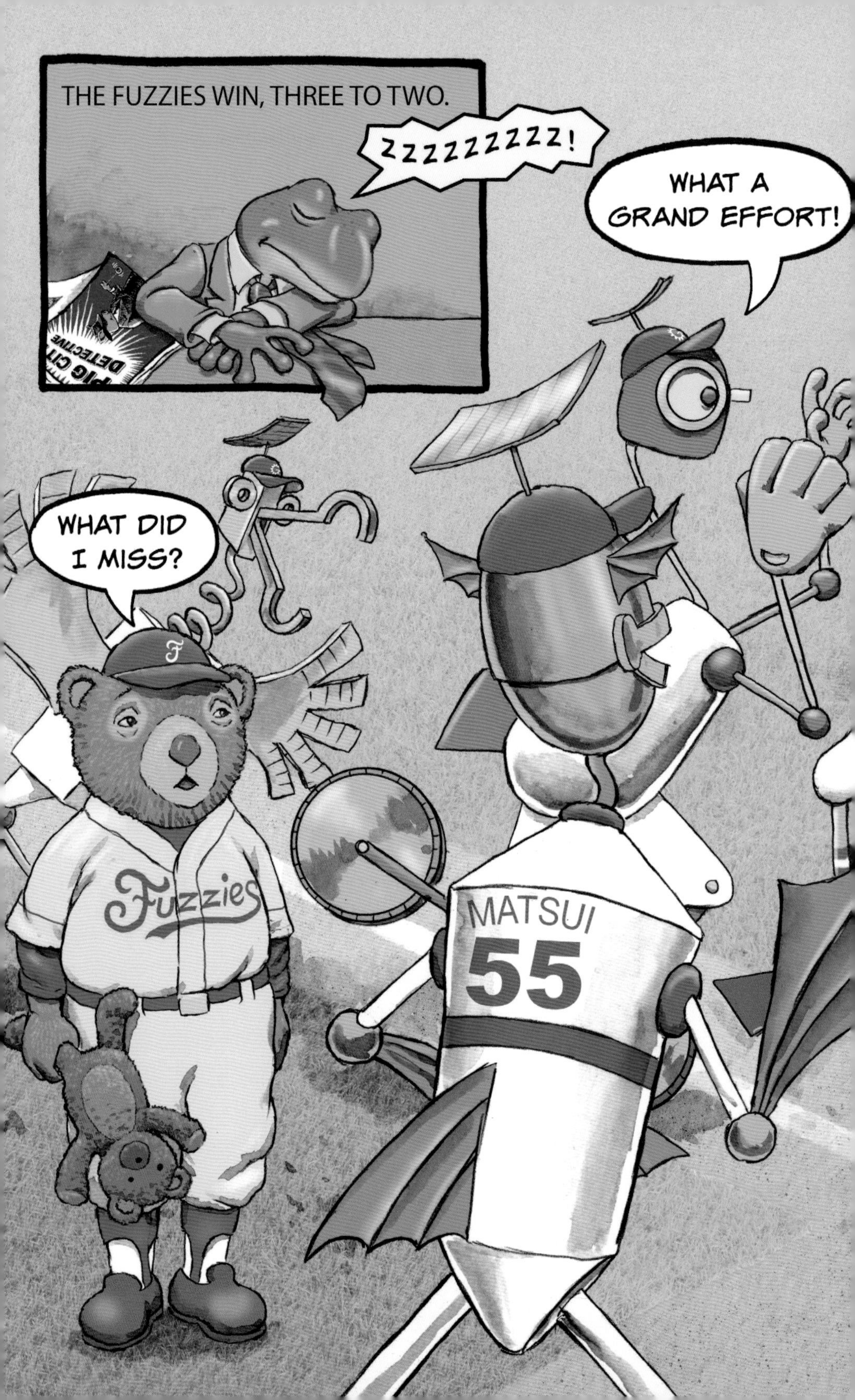
THE FUZZIES WIN, THREE TO TWO.
ZZZZZZZZZ!
WHAT A GRAND EFFORT!
WHAT DID I MISS?
Fuzzies
MATSUI
55

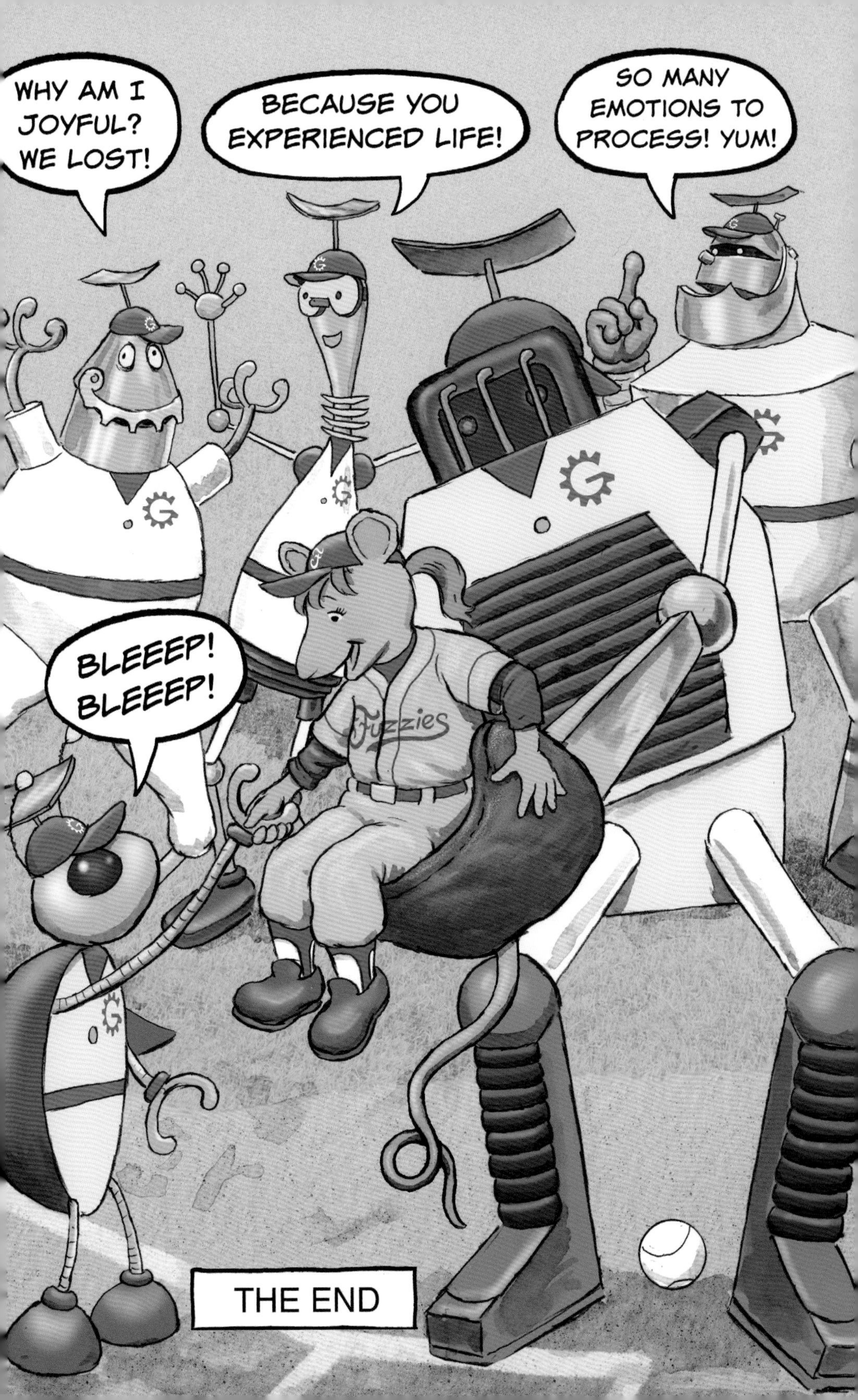
WHY AM I JOYFUL? WE LOST!
BECAUSE YOU EXPERIENCED LIFE!
SO MANY EMOTIONS TO PROCESS! YUM!
BLEEEP! BLEEEP!
Fuzzies
THE END

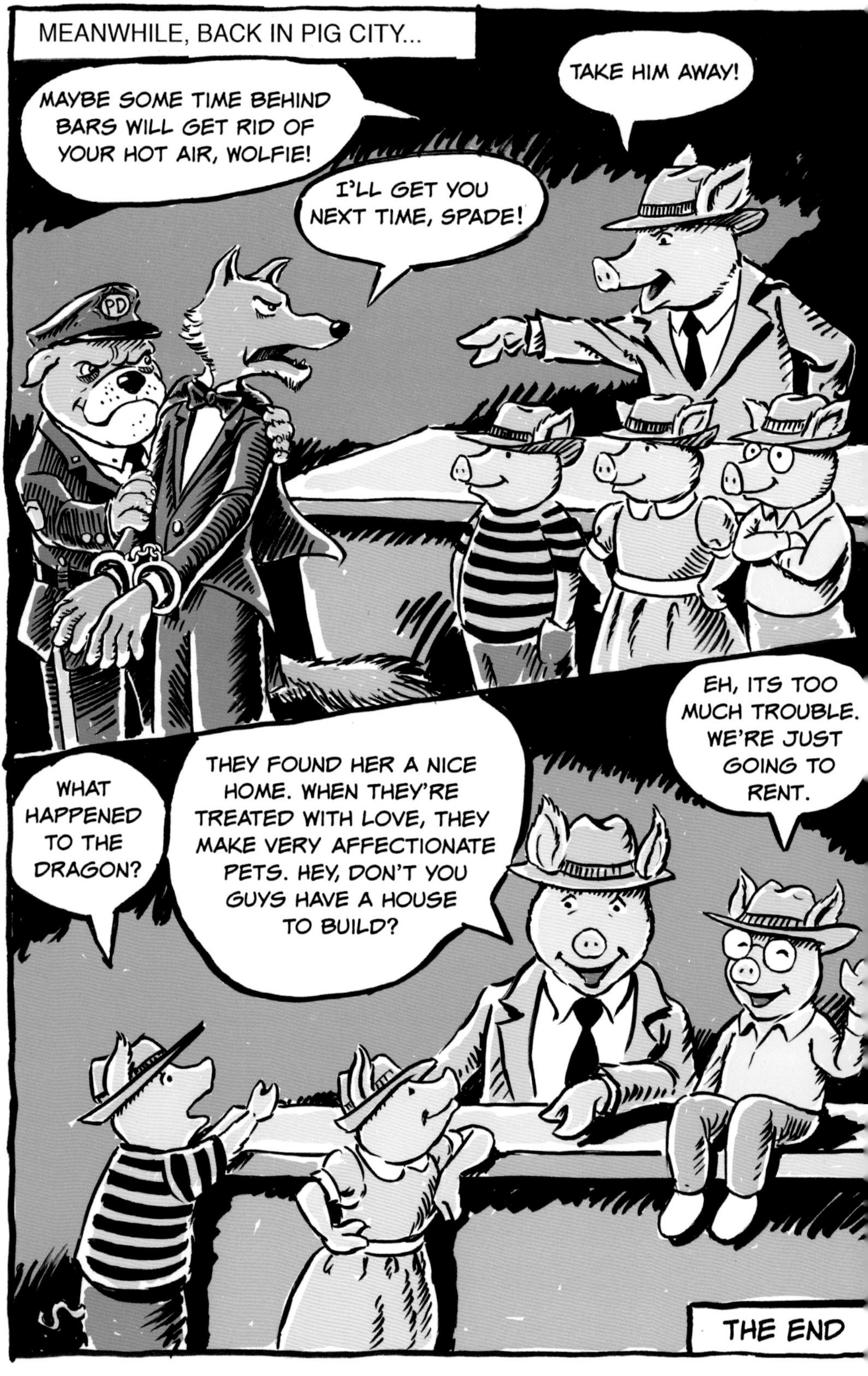
MEANWHILE, BACK IN PIG CITY...
MAYBE SOME TIME BEHIND BARS WILL GET RID OF YOUR HOT AIR, WOLFIE!
TAKE HIM AWAY!
I'LL GET YOU NEXT TIME, SPADE!
PD
WHAT HAPPENED TO THE DRAGON?
THEY FOUND HER A NICE HOME. WHEN THEY'RE TREATED WITH LOVE, THEY MAKE VERY AFFECTIONATE PETS. HEY, DON'T YOU GUYS HAVE A HOUSE TO BUILD?
EH, ITS TOO MUCH TROUBLE. WE'RE JUST GOING TO RENT.
THE END

A MEMO FROM THE COMMISIONER

As I was writing this book I had a lot of fun coming up with the names for the Geartown Clankees. Although some of the Fuzzies are named after actual players (Jackie Robinson and Sammy Sosa) every one of the Clankees are named after players from baseball history. The challenge was to find names that I could blend with words associated with engines, robots, or anything mechanical. I imagine that adults will groan as they read my puns, but I hope young readers will be curious enough to look up some of these baseball greats. I should add that the positions the characters play in this book do not necessarily correspond with the positions that they played in real life.
Here is a list of the actual players:

Harmon Killebrew, Lou Gehrig, Johnny Bench, Rogers Hornsby, Rusty Staub, Alex Rodriguez, Ty Cobb, Greg Luzinski, Bucky Dent, Cy Young, Mark McGwire, Honus Wagner, Kirby Puckett, Hank Aaron, Hideki Matsui

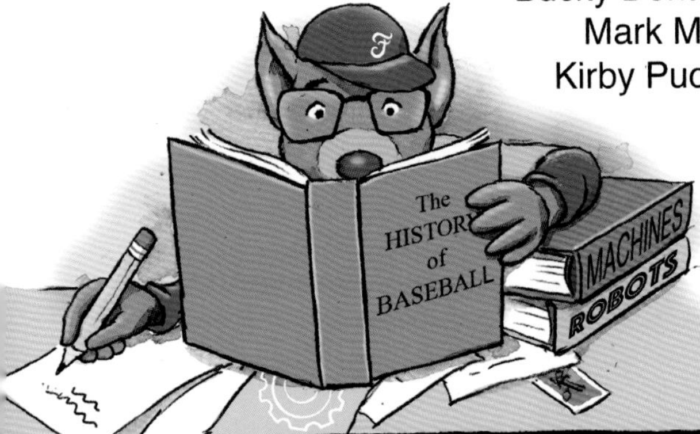
The
HISTOR
of
BASEBALL
MACHINES
ROBOTS

LEARN TO SPEAK ITALIAN WITH PERCIVALE PENGUINO

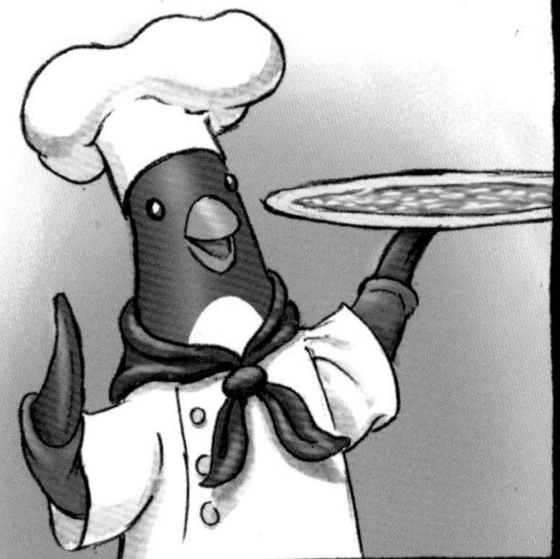

robot amichevoli – friendy robots

sfortuna – bad luck

posso giocare – I can play

THE FERNWOOD VALLEY FUZZIES

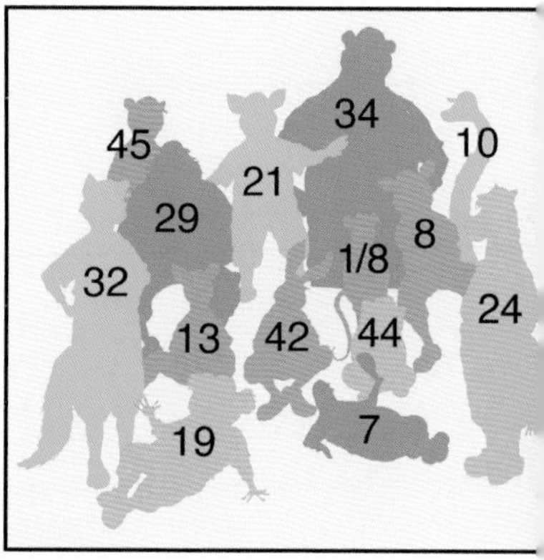
45
34
10
21
29
8
1/8
32
24
13
42
44
19
7

#1/8 Blossom Honey-Possum, Outfield
#7 Percivale Penguino, Outfield
#8 Pam the Lamb, Outfield
#10 Larry Boa, Third Base
#13 Pepe Perrito, Shortstop
#19 Kazuki Koala, Outfield
#21 Hammy Sosa, Catcher
#24 Pony Perez, Shortstop
#29 Red Kowasaki, Pitcher
#32 Sandy Kofox, Pitcher
#34 Bo Grizzly, First Base & Manager
#42 Jackie Rabbitson, Second Base
#44 Walter Wombat, Outfield
#45 Kit Ocelot, Pitcher

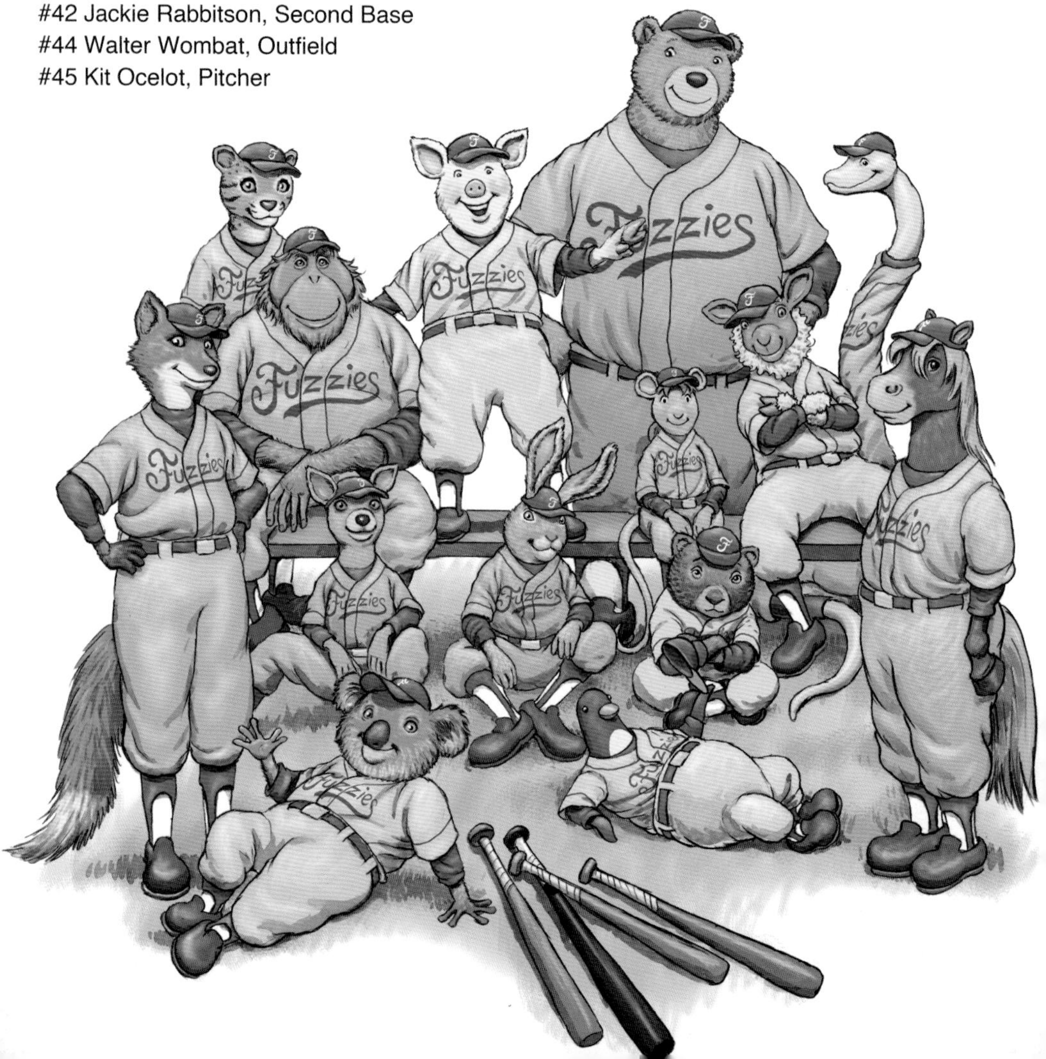

THE GEARTOWN CLANKEES

3 Harmon Kilowatt, third base
4 Lou Gearig, right field
5 Johnny Wrench, catcher
9 Rotor Hornsby, pitcher
10 Crusty Fob, left field
13 Axel Rod Regrease, shortstop
15 Ty Cog, left field
19 Greg Pluginsky, second base
20 Clunky Dent, Manager
24 Cyborg Young, pitcher
25 Spark McPlyer, first base
33 Honus Wingnut, right field
34 Kirby Sprocket, pitcher
44 Crank Aaron, center field
55 Techy Matsui, third base

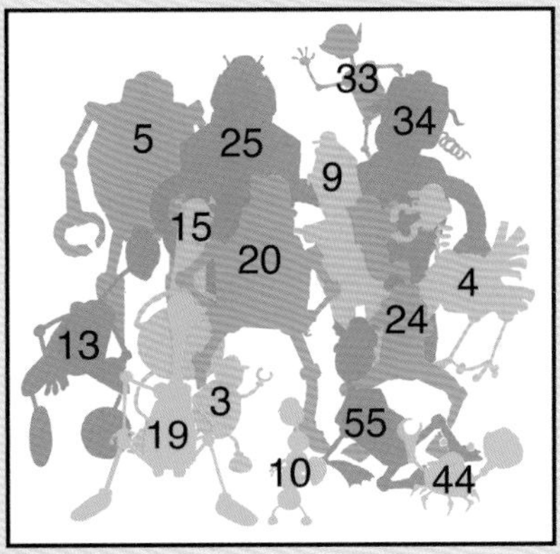
33
34
5
25
9
15
20
4
24
13
3
19
55
10
44

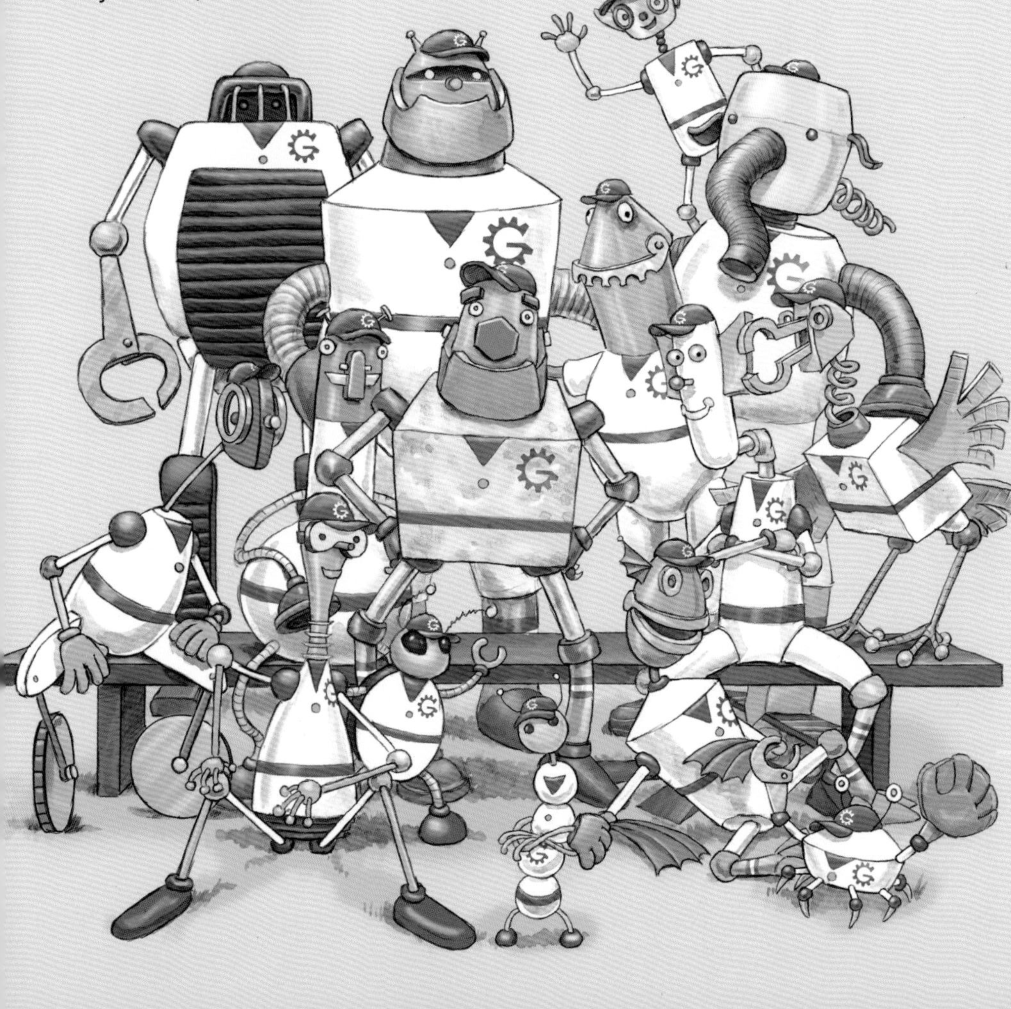

WATCH OUT FOR PAPERCUTZ™

Welcome to FUZZY BASEBALL #3 "RBI Robots" by John Steven Gurney, "The Commissioner," from Papercutz, those Fuzzy-fans in the cheap seats dedicated to publishing great graphic novels for all ages. I'm Jim Salicrup, Editor-in-Chief and former Assistant Coach for the Fernwood Valley Fuzzies. I'm really excited to announce that in addition to producing FUZZY BASEBALL graphic novels, as well as assembling all our other incredible graphic novels, we got some exciting exciting Papercutz publishing news—so exciting, it was even in the New York Times and The Hollywood Reporter! So exciting, I'm going to tell you all about it right now...

Papercutz has managed to get the North American rights to publish perhaps the most successful comics series in the world—ASTERIX! Now some of you may not have heard of this Asterix fella, so let's take a quick journey in the Papercutz time machine...

We're back in the year 50 BC in the ancient country of Gaul, located where France, Belgium, and the Southern Netherlands are today. All of Gaul has been conquered by the Romans... well, not all of it. One tiny village, inhabited by indomitable Gauls, resists the invaders again and again. That doesn't make it easy for the garrisons of Roman soldiers surrounding the village in fortified camps. So, how's it possible that a small village can hold its own against the mighty Roman Empire? The answer is this guy...

This is **Asterix**. A shrewd, little warrior of keen intellect... and superhuman strength. Asterix gets his superhuman strength from a magic potion. But he's not alone.

Obelix is Asterix's inseparable friend. He too has superhuman strength. He's a menhir (tall, upright stone monuments) deliveryman, he loves eating wild boar and getting into brawls. Obelix is always ready to drop everything to go off on a new adventure with Asterix.

Panoramix, the village's venerable Druid, gathers mistletoe and prepares magic potions. His greatest success is the power potion. When a villager drinks this magical elixir he or she is temporarily granted super-strength. This is just one of the Druid's potions! And now you know why this small village can survive, despite seemingly impossible odds. While we're here, we may as well meet a few other Gauls...

Cacofonix is the bard—the village poet. Opinions about his talents are divided: he thinks he's awesome, everybody else think he's awful, but when he doesn't say anything, he's a cheerful companion and well-liked...

Vitalstatistix, finally, is the village's chief. Majestic, courageous, and irritable, the old warrior is respected by his men and feared by his enemies. Vitalstatistix has only one fear: that the sky will fall on his head but, as he says himself, "That'll be the day!"

There are plenty more characters around here, but you've met enough for now. In other words, that's Gaul, folks! It's time we get back and wrap this up. Now, where did we put that time machine? Oh, there it is!

We're back, and we hope you enjoyed this trip back in time to explore 50 BC. For more information about ASTERIX and his upcoming Papercutz graphic novels, just go to papercutz.com. As for FUZZY BASEBALL, all we can say is, "Play Gaul—er, we mean BALL!"

Thanks,

Jim

STAY IN TOUCH!

EMAIL: salicrup@papercutz.com
WEB: papercutz.com
TWITTER: @papercutzgn
INSTAGRAM: @papercutzgn
FACEBOOK: PAPERCUTZGRAPHICNOVELS
REGULAR MAIL: Papercutz, 160 Broadway, Suite 700, East Wing, New York, NY 10038

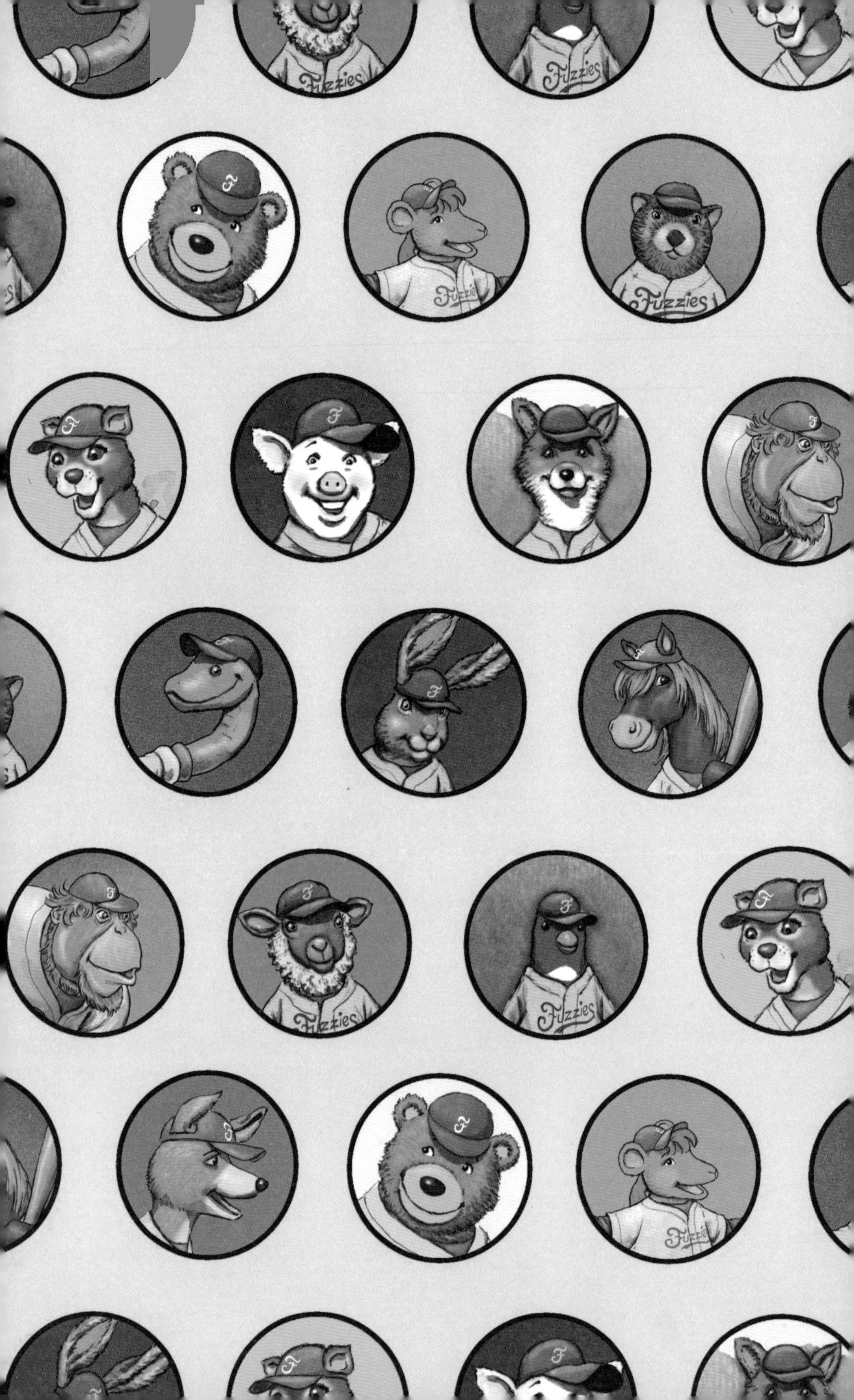
Fuzzies
Fuzzies
Fuzzies
Fuzzies
Fuzzies